Flat-Out Matt

Jessica Park

Flat-Out Matt

Matt is a junior at MIT. He's geeky, he's witty, he's brilliant.

And he's also very, very stupid.

When beautiful, cool, insightful Julie moves in with Matt's family, why (oh why!) does he pretend to be his absent brother Finn for her alleged benefit?

It seems harmless enough until her short-term stay becomes permanent. And until it snowballs into heart-squeezing insanity. And until he falls in love with Julie, and Julie falls in love with *Finn*.

But ... *Matt* is the right one for her. If only he can make Julie see it. Without telling her the truth, without shattering them all. Particularly his fragile sister Celeste, who may need Julie the most.

You saw Matt through Julie's eyes in FLAT-OUT LOVE. Now go deeper into Matt's world in this FLAT-OUT MATT novella. Live his side of the story, break when his heart breaks, and fall for the unlikely hero all over again.

Take an emotional skydive for two prequel chapters and seven FLAT-OUT LOVE chapters retold from his perspective, and then land with a brand-new steamy finale chapter from Julie.

Author's Note

Two chapters, The Sleepover and Keep Going, contain more mature content than *Flat-Out Love* (Keep Going, in particular), and were written based on reader demand. They wouldn't have fit in well with the original *Flat-Out Love*, but given that this is a fan-driven companion novella, I think they work. While the content here is upped at bit, the scenes are tastefully done. (So, you know, sorry to those of you who wanted lewd and graphic stuff.)

Dedication

Flat-Out Matt is dedicated to the fans who believed in Matt and who fell in love with this unlikely hero. This book is for you, from Matt, with his eternal gratitude (and embarrassment) at becoming a "book boyfriend" for so many readers.

This is also for geeky guys everywhere who are finally getting the positive attention they deserve. And maybe a little action.

Table of Contents

In This Together

A *Flat-Out Love* Prequel Chapter

Matt Watkins is visible only in infrared.

Finn Watkins I WOULD LIKE TO ANNOUNCE A STRATEGIC ALLIANCE BETWEEN YOUR FACE AND MY ASS, INVOLVING A LOT OF KISSING.

Matt set his backpack down and retrieved a water bottle. It was in the mid-forties today on Mount Washington, so the water had stayed blessedly cold. They'd already done one hike today, and now they were in the midst of their second. Matt was sweaty, achy, and tired, and his feet hurt like hell. This was only the second time that he'd worn these hiking boots, and he knew that his feet were starting to blister. But he wouldn't change a thing. When a third of the water was gone, he returned it to the backpack.

"C'mon, dude!" Finn shouted from twenty yards ahead. "We made it through the Fan. Keep going!" He lifted his sunglasses, rested them in his hair, and grinned. Finn was in his element.

The brothers were on the eastern side of the mountain, on the Huntington Ravine Trail that led to the base of an eight-hundred-foot headwall, and then to the steep slabs and ledges of Central Gully. It wasn't a particularly difficult route at this time of year, but inexperienced climbers with bad judgment and little (or wrong) equipment could easily get into plenty of trouble during the winter months. Snow rangers had rescued more than one ill-prepared climber from this area.

Even without the danger factor that they both loved, Matt and Finn liked this hike. It had every sort of terrain, and they had already gone over large boulders, through rocky scrub, and across a small stream. Some sections, like the Fan, were scree fields, covered with dirt and gravel that could easily make hikers lose their footing. Even Finn wasn't crazy about crossing those in wet weather, but they had dry air and sunshine today. They now had to tackle the ledges that would take them to Pinnacle Gully, and this next leg of climbing would be all about finding the perfect crevice for their hands to grip and relying on the high-quality soles of their boots.

Matt reached his brother. "Okay, I'm ready."

Finn squinted in the sunshine, his blond hair nearly glowing in the light. "You sure? Let's just sit for a few minutes. Enjoy the view a bit." Before Matt could stop him, Finn sat on a slab of rock surrounded by grassy patches. "Besides, we should eat again. This right here is the food of champions." He pulled a plastic bag of granola, dried fruit, and chocolate chips from his backpack and held it out to Matt while he rummaged for the beef jerky. "We should get Mom to serve this for dinner. Even she couldn't ruin trail mix, right?"

Matt sat down a few feet away and adjusted the brim of his hat, shielding his eyes from the sun. "I wouldn't count on that. I'm quite sure that she could do something irrevocably awful. Perhaps pulverize everything in a blender and serve us a bowl of dust for dinner?"

"We could just snort it through straws!" Finn let out his typical loud, infectious laugh. "Let's not suggest this to her because she'd do it for sure." He leaned back on his elbows. "Damn, Matty, would you look at that view. The mountains, the trees, the perfect sky. What more could you ask for?"

"Not much," Matt agreed. He watched his brother, well aware of how deeply and unabashedly he idolized Finn. Finn, who could do just about anything, and knew how to handle the world with excessive competence and charm. Finn had all the social finesse that Matt knew he never would. Not to mention Finn's annoying good looks, made even more attractive by how unaware he was of his flawlessness. Even minor things, like the fact that Finn's hiking pants fell in a somehow cool style while Matt's legs looked the same as they did in any pants. It was endearing and exasperating.

Finn's face was flushed from the cold, which just added to his vibrant aura. "I know this is a pretty easy trip for us. Hope you don't mind."

"Not at all. But why did you want to do this? We could handle this in our sleep."

"I just... wanted to hang out with you. It's kind of hard to chat when we're hang gliding, you know?" Finn cupped his hands over his mouth. "Maaaattty! How are youuuuuuu?"

"Okay, fair enough."

"So, little brother, let's hear about this girlfriend of yours. It's your senior year of high school, you've got a sweet lady to sneak into the house at night, and I'm not living at home to help cover for you. So how's it going?"

Matt rolled his eyes. "Everything is fine. I'm well aware of the creaky steps and how to get past Mom and Dad's room without them hearing."

"I trained you well." Finn was clearly pleased. "Now, give me dirt. I have yet to meet this lovely creature, and all I know is that her name is Ellen and she's shooting to get into Yale for next fall."

"Both true."

"And how did you two lovebirds meet?" Finn said, batting his eyelashes.

"Ellen and I were both selected to run an afterschool group for those who needed help with molecular biophysics and biochemistry. A number of students have been taking college courses to bulk up their resumes, so we've been tutoring them twice a week."

"Scintillating. Tell me something more exciting than that. What's she like? Is she funny? Do you love her?" Finn cocked his head to the side and overemphasized every word. "Do you *make* sweet love to her?"

"She's going to major in Women's, Gender, and Sexuality Studies, if that answers your question."

"It doesn't answer my question. That either means that she's too uptight to do it so she just reads about it, or..."

Matt smiled. "She's not too uptight."

Finn flopped back onto the ground and rubbed his eyes with his hands. "Oh my God, my baby brother is engaging in sordid activities with a woman he's not married to! Or even engaged! It's disgusting! Why didn't you tell me about this sooner? Maybe I could have prevented this vile behavior. It's all my fault. I'll never forgive myself for failing to secure your virginity until you were of age."

"Finn, shut up. You've been engaging in sordid activities with quite a number of women. And I'm pretty sure some of the things you've done are illegal in a few states."

"Damn straight they are!" He clapped his hands together and looked at Matt. "I'm a sophomore in college, what do you expect? Seriously, so things are, uh, good between you and this unspeakably loose Ellen character?"

Matt nodded and fiddled with the bag in his hands.

"I see you trying not to smile," Finn teased. "I'm happy for you. And she sounds just as nauseatingly academic as you are. Tell me more."

"She's hoping to spend the summer interning for a Harvard professor who is researching—"

"That's not what I mean. Tell me more about *her*. You and her. You care about her? Does she make you laugh? Is she warm, and girly, and sexy, and sweet?"

"Of course I care about her. She's very smart and focused, and Ellen is extremely supportive of my plan to double-major."

"Well," Finn said, clearing his throat, "she sounds just wonderful."

"What's that condescension for?"

"Nothing. It's just...." Finn popped a handful of granola into his mouth and kept talking. "I want you to have fun."

"I am having fun."

"In a controlled, regimented fashion, yes. But I think you could have more fun. It wouldn't hurt you to hook up with someone a little less like our mother."

"What an atrocious, puke-inducing thing to say."

"Go date some girl with purple hair and tattoos. Someone emotional and funny and interested in you for something other than your book smarts. Someone who'd jump out of an airplane with you. You could give a lot more to a relationship than what I suspect you're giving this Ellen chick. And you could get more, too. You deserve it."

"Ellen and I are on the same page when it comes to a lot of important things. We have similar life goals, value the same social policies.... There is a lot of respect between us."

"Ah, yes, the stuff great love stories are made of. I'm overwhelmed by the romance. Live a little, Matthew. Get a B instead of an A+ in a class because you're so passionately in love and busy schtupping your brains out that you didn't have time to study."

"That's you, Finn, not me."

"It *is* you. You just have to let it happen. You'd love it."

"I'm quite happy with Ellen."

"You're bored with Ellen. I know you. You'll skydive, and hang into ravines by thin ropes, and go rafting in the rapids, but you won't... what? Get crazy and reckless with an amazing girl? You won't fall madly out-of-your-brains in love? Let your world as you know it be blown to bits because you fall heart-crushingly head-over-heels for someone?"

Matt laughed. "You go enjoy your tattooed nymphomaniacs, and I'll be just fine the way I am."

"I knew Ellen was uptight," Finn muttered.

Matt laughed. "She's not uptight! I'll have you know that we... do it plenty."

"Yeah, fine. At least there's that."

"And it's not like there's anything wrong with both of us focusing on school. You care about that, too, considering that you're not exactly failing out of Brandeis."

"True, but I'm not you, that's for sure. You've got something that I could never have."

"Yeah, right."

"It's true. Dude, you need to appreciate how goddamn gifted you are. You're so smart that I don't understand what you're talking about half the time, and we all know how brilliant *I* am." Finn winked. "Matty, you're amazing."

He shook his head. Finn was laying it on thick. "Yes, I know how I'm smart and how I'm not."

"What are you not good at? You're going to MIT next year. It doesn't get any more genius than that."

Matt sighed. "It's not that. Fine, yes, if I get into MIT, I'll do well there. We all know that." He looked up and took in the skyline.

Finn was quiet for a while and Matt could feel his brother's stare piercing into him.

Finally Matt looked over. "What? What is it?"

"Aw, Matt, knock it off. No one in the world could have as amazing a brother as I do. You've got a heart and a spirit like nobody else. Please try to remember that. You're more than just the smart one."

"I know that. I do. I'm also the hot brother." Matt tossed the trail mix bag at Finn, hitting him smack in the head. "Sometimes I just need you to remind me."

"Look who's all cocky now, huh? Got the girl, got the fancy-pants college that's going to chase after you for sure.... What's next for you?" Finn asked.

Matt hung his arms over his knees and surveyed the skyline. He smiled. "I don't know. But I can't wait to find out."

Finn got up and walked the few steps to stand near his brother. "I can't wait either. I'm proud of you, man. I really am. Things are good for us now, huh?"

Matt hesitated. "Yes."

Finn frowned. "What is it? Is it Celeste? Is she okay?"

"She's great. I mean, she misses you, of course, but that's normal."

The truth was that Celeste hated that Finn lived in the dorms. She had a tendency to get overly irritable with Matt, clearly for not being as in tune with elementary school children as his brother. He did the best that he could with her and tried to engage her in activities he thought she would enjoy. So far his attempt to ignite interest in his mineral club had not gone over well, and had only produced a rather bemused, "Oh, Matty." But he wasn't about to follow Finn's lead and waste a Saturday at that horrible Canobie Lake amusement park. He had no tolerance for the crowds, and lines, and the awful blaring music that was piped over loudspeakers. The idiotic rides held no appeal and he couldn't understand why anyone found a day there to be anything but grotesque. As far as Matt was concerned, it was American culture at its worst. Finn, on the other hand, braved the insanity a few times a year, and he and Celeste always returned home with an armful of cheaply made neon-colored stuffed animals that Finn had won for her. Thank God that Finn was around to give their sister the fun that she needed. Matt wished he knew how, and he envied Finn's ability to become so childlike at a moment's notice. Finn could play, and giggle, and swoop Celeste up in his arms with such ease. Maybe when she was older he would be a better big brother. He'd figure out a way so that she would love him the way that she loved Finn.

Matt smiled. "It's good that you come over every Sunday and hang out with her. She admires the hell out of you."

"I miss that munchkin, I really do. Is she not the happiest damn kid you've ever seen? I don't suppose our parents would let her move into the dorm with me, do you?"

"Probably not. Besides, she's a lousy beer funneler. Gets halfway through and starts gagging. Very unseemly."

"Useless ten-year-olds. Fine, you get her to practice a little more, maybe with a nice lager ale, and I'll work on Mom and Dad."

"You and Celeste are going to abandon me and leave me alone in that house of horrors?" Matt tossed up his hands. "Thanks. I appreciate the support."

Finn paused and set his hands on his hips. "What's going on, Matt?"

Matt thought for a moment, trying to figure out if he should say anything. "Mom is not... right. I don't know how to explain it. She pulls it together when you come home, but...."

"It's happening again."

Matt nodded. "I think so. I can't keep track of the ups and downs."

"Aw, hell." Finn picked up a small rock and stood, hurling it as far as he could over the side of the mountain. "Is she off her meds?"

"I'm not sure. Maybe."

"I know she doesn't like them." Finn paced in the small rock area behind Matt. "She told me they flatten her moods too much, but I don't think she has a choice."

Matt listened to Finn's muttering and sighing, and heard him kick some pebbles.

"What's Dad doing about this?" Finn asked.

"What do you think?"

"His usual ineffective grin-and-bear-it method?"

"Yup. She certainly doesn't make it easy for him, though. I don't know that I blame him."

"You should blame him. He's got children to worry about. He's got responsibilities." Finn sighed again and swore under his breath. "You'll be out of there soon enough, Matt."

"And what about Celeste?"

"She'll be funneling at keg parties with me, remember?" Finn hurled another rock. "I know, I know. Not funny. You're right, of course."

"Celeste isn't wired like Mom. She is exhaustively cheerful all the time. I wouldn't want to see that change."

"No," Finn said firmly. "We're not going to let them take that from her. We won't."

"Maybe you could talk to Mom? She'll listen to you. She responds to you the most."

"Knock it off with that talk. That's not true."

"It's okay, Finn. Really. It's how it's always been. "

"You don't get it, Matt, do you?"

"Get what?"

"The reason that she's tougher on you is because she sees you as competition. You're smarter than she is, and she can't stand that." Finn plopped down next to Matt again. "She's jealous. Plain and simple."

"Huh. You think?"

"She's always going to be harder on you to try to bring you down a notch or two. I love Mom, but... ignore her garbage. I know she is giving you a hard time about MIT, telling you that you won't get enough of a well-rounded education. But that's not true. She could never get in there, and she knows that you will. You're going to do fantastic things." He sat down again next to Matt and beamed. "It's gonna be fun to watch."

"Thanks." Matt dropped his head and fussed with his shoelace. "Thanks, Finn."

"What about Celeste? What do you think she'll do with her life?"

"Maybe she'll stick with the piano? Or something else creative. Can't you picture her as an artist of some sort? We'll go to her gallery showings and listen to her explain the symbolism found in some bizarre sculpture that she's spent months forming out of pinecones and zippers."

"Totally," Finn agreed. "It'll be weird and wonderful."

"Yes, it will."

"Just like her. Yeah, she's a little too smart for her own good and not exactly like all of the other kids at her school, but she's got potential to do something great, too. Something really unique and outstanding. Don't you think?"

Matt nodded. "I couldn't agree more."

"Can you imagine her as a teenager?" Finn groaned. "Ugh, it's only a few years away. That mess of blonde hair is going to have the boys knocking down the front door."

"No kidding. We'll have to set up some sort of security system. I'll take care of the background checks, and you can rig the booby traps. I'm thinking something to do with nets and pulleys?"

Finn high-fived Matt. "Deal."

"So, you'll talk to Mom?"

"Yeah. Don't worry about anything. I'm going to fix this."

"You and your *Don't Worry, I'm a Jedi* shirt?" Matt smiled.

"With a little help from you and your *Friends Don't Let Friends Drink and Derive* shirt."

"You don't need me, Finn."

"I do need you, Matt. You're my best friend, and we're in this together."

Matt's shoelace continued to be in desperate need of attention. "I love you, Finn."

Finn laughed and threw his arm around Matt's neck, pulling him in close. "Aw, Matty, you big sap. I love you, too, bro." He held him tight for a few moments. "Everything is going to be just fine. I promise."

Matt nodded. "Should we get going?"

Finn squeezed his arm around Matt one more time. "Yup. Let's do it."

They both put on their backpacks, and Matt turned to take in the spectacular view one more time before he started focusing on getting up the steeper slabs of rock ahead of them. This wasn't a challenging climb for the two of them now, but the winter months would bring excellent opportunity for ice climbing here.

"Hey, Finn?"

Finn raised the hood of his fleece over his head. "Yeah?"

"We should come back here when we've got ice."

"Dude, I'm so all over that. We'll get new equipment for Christmas! New ropes, new ice axe.... We need a really good weather tracker, too. Did you know Mount Washington has some of the craziest weather anywhere? Unpredictable. Changes in a flash."

"That's the fun, right?" Matt followed Finn over the craggy rock.

"Well, yeah. But we're going to be careful. Right now, this is only a Class 3 climb. Throw in snow, ice, and God knows what kind of weather? Total game changer. There are a few different gully options to ascend. We'll have to be smart about this."

"That's unfortunate, since neither of us is too bright."

"I know. Especially you. Tragic." Finn looked back and winked at Matt. "Tragic."

They hiked for a bit and then Finn stopped, steadied his footing, and pointed off to the right. "There. That's our ravine. What do you say, Matty? February? Give ourselves a real challenge."

"They do say February is the harshest month."

"And by *harshest* they mean *best*."

"Hell, yeah," Matt said.

"So you're in?"

"I'm in," Matt agreed. He took in the sight of his brother, totally at ease on this terrain, the sun reflecting off the rock onto Finn's eager face. He would go anywhere with Finn. Drop-off cliffs, gnarled jungles, deep oceans.... Matt would be safe and loved. Matt would be treasured. "All in."

Finn let out a joyous whoop and raised both hands triumphantly in the air. "See ya in February! We're coming for you! Me and my brother, you hear me? Me and my brother."

He turned and winked at Matt.

#FlatFinnSaves

A *Flat-Out Love* Prequel Chapter

Matt Watkins Machine time a in polarity the reverse to how know anyone does: question quick?

"Please, Celeste. *Please.*" Matt couldn't keep the pleading tone from his voice. It had become impossible to muster anything resembling a happy—or even neutral—tone when talking to his sister. Every word he spoke to her was loaded with begging, cajoling, or frustration. Sometimes anger.

Matt leaned against the wall that led into the living room. The girl before him was too despondent for him to look at, so he focused on the plate in his hand. Staring at the stinky meatball sub was preferable to looking at his sister. Celeste was seated on the end of the couch, her legs pulled in tightly to her chest, and her arms wrapped around them with her hands clenched together. She hadn't cried in weeks. In fact, she hadn't done much of anything in weeks. At least school was out now, so the morning grind of trying to get her functional enough to get to class was on hiatus. But now the days seemed endless. There was nothing to fill them with. Everything had a downside. Everything *was* a downside. Maybe he missed the crying, the noise, the reactions, because Celeste's near-silence was worse. Her expressionless, stoic face destroyed him again and again. At least there was still something left to be destroyed. *Ah, an upside!* Matt thought bitterly.

He forced himself to rally. Again. He crossed the room and sat down next to her. "You need to eat. I got you a sub from that unsanitary hole-in-the-wall place that you like." Matt set the plate on the coffee table.

How much longer could he do this? It had been five months since Finn died. Five months and twelve days. Erin and Roger were barely holding it together as it was, so they were of minimal help. Matt understood how it was nearly impossible to see past your own grief to deal with somebody else's, but he was doing it, for God's sake. Couldn't they help him? Couldn't *somebody* help him? Evidently not. Yes, Celeste allowed him to take her to and from school, she did her homework, she ate (when he made her), and she could sometimes engage in watered-down conversation. But there was no healing. He was going to have to think of something.

Matt brushed her hair from her face and set a pile of curls behind her shoulder. "I should take you to get another haircut soon, huh?" Matt paused, waiting for a response that wasn't going to come. "Baby girl, please."

Celeste continued looking out the window. "Do not call me that, Matthew."

Matt sighed. "I'm sorry, I didn't mean—"

"That is what *he* called me, and I do not want to hear those two words adjoined like that. Especially from you."

He had to give her credit. She really knew how to drive the knife in further.

The smell of the sub was churning his stomach. Granted, everything seemed to churn his stomach, but today it was worse. "Come on. Eat." He managed to strengthen his voice, wanting to sound as directive as he could. "It's not a choice. We eat, we sleep, we keep going."

She turned from her spot and looked at the coffee table. She stayed still for a long moment. *A standoff between Celeste and the sandwich*, Matt thought. *Who would win this battle of wills? Who would claim victory? The tension was great...*

"Just. Eat. Stop thinking and eat." Matt put the plate in her lap. Maybe he could distract her and just shove food into her mouth without her noticing? That would be easier than this ritual of negotiation they always had to go through. "Finn would never want you like this." It was a cheap shot, he knew, but, like Celeste, he wasn't above that these days.

Celeste glared at him, but she did pick up the sandwich.

Ha! Small victories.

They sat uncomfortably as Matt oversaw her eating. He knew if he left the room that she would stop and probably spit out whatever was in her mouth.

"So, look, you have a birthday coming up in a few weeks. What should we do to celebrate?"

"There will not be a celebration, Matthew."

"We have to do something. *I* want to do something. How about dinner out? Or we could see if any of the theater groups have productions running now. I'd love to see a show with you. And is there a particular gift you'd like? I have a few things for you, and Mom and Dad, too, of course." That wasn't exactly a lie since he had bought her some gifts on their behalf.

"I do not see a compelling reason to acknowledge the day as anything but another insignificant, if not torturous, twenty-four period. Do you?" she asked accusingly. "Do you, Matthew?" She shoved the plate with the now half-eaten sandwich across the table and lay on the couch.

Matt rubbed his eyes. He simply didn't have the energy to do this with her right now. The cycle was all too familiar to him; he'd spend twenty minutes trying to be animated and kind and (if he was really trying harder than usual) funny, and she'd either be totally silent or heartbreakingly abusive. Then he would try to reason with her, tap into any part of her that still *lived*, then get angry and say something that he'd regret. But today, he wasn't strong enough. He reached into his pocket and pulled out his wallet. "Here." He tossed a credit card on the table as he stood. "Go online and buy yourself whatever you want. You should have something nice, especially this year. Do it for me, for yourself, for Finn.... I don't care who. Just do it."

Matt walked out of the room.

****

The screen glowed brightly in the dark of Matt's room, and he just now noticed that evening had set in. He unconsciously glanced at the calendar on his laptop. Five months, twenty-six days. *Stop counting, stop counting.* He lifted the next bill from the pile and arranged an online payment. While everything else in the house had fallen to shit, at least there was money in his parents' account. When the electricity had been turned off because Roger and Erin forgot the two shut-off notices that had come in the mail, Matt had offered to deal with the bills. At least the loss of power had presented him and his parents with a conversation topic. A sterile and unhappy one, but it provided an excuse for interaction. Aside from specific logistical issues that had to be dealt with, no one talked to each other, and no one made much eye contact. Certainly no one smiled.

He scrolled through the checking account, confirming that everything was normal and then did the same for the credit cards. He let out a small smile for only the second time in ages. It was hard not to feel a brief moment of levity when he'd first seen the charge last week. A little over a hundred dollars had been charged to an online party shop. Celeste had gone ahead and bought herself something, presumably the makings of a birthday party. She must have come around to the idea of the family celebrating her birthday in some form. It was probably just a mess of decorations, and all likely done from some sense of obligation to Finn's memory, but Matt didn't care. For the first time since that ungodly awful day last February, Celeste had done *something* positive.

When the last bill was scheduled for payment, Matt collected the papers, ran them through a shredder, and sat back. He knew it was inexcusable that he was in charge of this, but it was much less complicated to simply tackle what had to be done than to try and get his own parents to handle this right now. It wouldn't be forever. Mom was doing... well, she was making progress. Dad had to focus on his wife, so Matt would hold down the rest of the fort until life got back to normal. Or whatever normal was going to be.

He lifted an envelope from his desk and sighed heavily. The letter was from MIT. This could have been, *should* have been, the one saving grace in what was otherwise a cyclone of misery. At least the admissions office was exceedingly understanding about his situation, and Matt had been able to defer for a year. Had he told his parents about this yet? He wasn't sure. But now what did he have to look forward to? A year at home in this entirely depressing environment? This house where no one was allowed in? There was always the possibility of auditing a few classes, but he certainly couldn't take on a full course load until things... settled.

Well, it wasn't really about him. It was about Celeste. And while ordering herself birthday party paraphernalia was a nice act, it didn't exactly signal a monumental leap out of depression. Celeste was just as dreadfully shut down as ever, and no amount of effort on Matt's part had made a difference. He was missing something. He had to be. There was a way to unlock the old Celeste.

Finn would know what that was, but Matt didn't.

His brother would be horribly disappointed in what Matt considered his near-total failure in managing Celeste. But he didn't know what else to do, how to cheer her up, how to glue together what was left of her. God *damn* Finn. He had always been so well thought-out. A risk taker, yes, but always with a solid understanding of the danger. He prepared, he planned, he executed smartly. Finn had never spontaneously hopped into a raft and ridden haphazardly down an unknown river. Daring acts always came with a level head.

So why had he jumped into the backseat of Erin's car that day? How could he have done something so stupid? He should have been less rash. Finn could have gotten into the front seat, couldn't he? And then pulled the emergency brake twenty feet from the house? He could have done something besides allowing Erin to career around on icy roads. Of course, it was easy for Matt to run through hundreds of alternatives. That was the nature of things like this, wasn't it? The gift that keeps on giving. Hours, days, *years*, of agonizing thinking ahead of him.

Gee, the future just looked brighter and brighter all the time.

The doorbell rang. Matt frowned. Who in the world could that be? As he started for the door, he heard the surprising sound of Celeste's footsteps tear out of her room and down the stairs. And even more shocking, the sound of absolute jubilation as she yelled out, "He's here! He's here!" She couldn't possibly have invited someone over, could she?

He stopped at the top of the stairs and listened, but the conversation lasted mere seconds before Celeste slammed the door. Only one set of footsteps thundered through the entryway and into the kitchen.

"Matty! Matty! You must witness the grand reveal! You must be here for... for the unveiling! Everything is going to turn around."

Unnerved by the now-uncharacteristic thrill in his sister's voice, he made his way hesitantly into the kitchen. No guest was with her, but Celeste looked undeniably happy. Her eyes were bright and her face flushed with excitement. She stood in the center of the kitchen, hands on both cheeks, staring at the large rectangular shipping box on the floor. Considering how long and flat the package was, Matt had to wonder what sort of party supply this could be. More importantly, what had she ordered that had lifted her spirits so dramatically? Well, whatever it was, Matt was damn happy it was here.

As he opened his mouth to speak, Matt realized that he didn't know how to address this version of Celeste. Speaking to a happy girl had become unfamiliar to him. He watched as she rummaged in a drawer and located a pair of scissors.

"I am going to use significant caution as I remove the tape that is sealing these edges. Cuts, tears, and other tragedies would be a result of my rushing ahead. I cannot let my enthusiasm impair my performance."

"What...uh..." Matt cleared his throat. "What do you have there, Celeste?"

She knelt down, poised with open scissors, as she assessed the package. "I am having difficulty determining how to approach this." Celeste looked at Matt, real happiness in her eyes. "Would you please assist me? My hands appear to be trembling, and I would not want to ruin this moment with an injury inflicted upon myself or him."

Who the hell was *him*? Who cared right now? Celeste was interacting with him, reaching out to him in a way she hadn't in months. He noted that it was now impossible to ignore that her speech patterns had become noticeably more odd over the past few months. He hadn't had much of an opportunity to hear her voice given how little she'd had to say recently, but he shrugged it off. He was just pleased to see her so animated.

"Yeah. I... I guess so. You've got me curious." He walked to her side and squatted down next to her.

Celeste handed him the scissors. "Now, you must promise to use the utmost care when severing the packaging. Okay? Okay, Matty?"

He smiled at her. "Sure. Of course I will."

Matt confidently slid the scissors between the folds of the brown cardboard. It must be some sort of giant poster, although considering the cost, he was pretty sure she'd completely overpaid. No matter. It was nice to be doing anything with his sister that didn't involve stony silence, cutting comments, or catatonia.

"There! You have done it!" Celeste announced. "I will lift the top off myself. I do so appreciate your assistance with this." She took her hand and placed it on Matt's knee.

Matt took his hand and put it on top of hers, looking at her with curiosity.

Celeste lifted her face and flashed a smile. "This is going to make a profound difference. Everything is about to change, Matthew. I am flooded with genuine anticipation and optimism."

"Then... then so am I," Matt agreed. "Let's see what you bought yourself."

"It's not an *it*," she said, clearly affronted, and she pulled a long, flat shape from the folds of the shipping cardboard. Celeste lifted up the object as she stood. "It's a *him*."

Matt felt his stomach tighten and his pulse pick up

"Oh my God, Celeste." He wasn't smiling anymore. "What have you done? *What* have you done?"

Matt started to shake his head back and forth, struggling to understand. In front of him stood a flat, life-sized cutout photograph of Finn.

The prodigal son returns.

Celeste had positioned some sort of flap near its feet so that this creepy replica of his brother stood on its own. She stepped back and admired her purchase. "Matthew, meet Flat Finn. Flat Finn, meet Matthew." She spun to face Matt and waited expectantly.

He could feel his whole body beginning to tremble, and he continued shaking his head.

Celeste wrinkled her nose in irritation and whispered in Matt's direction. "I believe that it is considered polite to introduce yourself or to otherwise impart some words of greeting upon meeting someone for the first time."

What did she want him to say? *Oh, good. Finn's home! At last!* All he could do was feel positively ill. He was surrounded by pain all the time, and now he was being asked to converse with this... this nightmare version of his dead brother? It was hard enough to look at pictures of Finn without being overwhelmed with grief, but this was too much. It was too crazy.

"No. No way, Celeste." Although he spoke slowly, his voice was harsh. "Get it out."

"What? What is the matter?" She took a step closer to Flat Finn.

"You're not doing this. Get rid of it. Why would you want that? Why?"

Celeste's face fell. "I do not understand why you are so angry with me. You are not responding the way I had envisioned you would."

"You thought I would like this? God! Wh...what exactly do you plan on doing with this thing?"

"It is not a thing. *He* is Flat Finn. He is going to be my sidekick and accompany me as I participate in daily activities. Flat Finn will watch over me as I sleep, he will have a place at the dinner table, and I have a feeling that he will be quite helpful with my history homework." She leaned her head in closer to the picture, positioning her ear by the mouth in the photograph. "Oh." She giggled. "He says that he has arrived to rescue me, just like the real Finn would do if he could. That is very kind of him. Matt, this is symbolism at its finest, I believe. Flat Finn will stay with me as a representative of my real brother."

"*I'm* your real brother!" Matt could hear himself screaming now. "I'm real! I'm here!"

"I... I... I know that, Matthew. I did not mean to imply—"

Matt moved swiftly across the room and grabbed the cardboard cutout with both hands. Celeste had gone insane. This was going into the trash right now.

"No! NO! Matty, no!" Celeste grabbed Matt's arm and dug her feet into the floor. "I need him!"

"No way. You are not doing this to yourself. Or to Mom and Dad. I'm putting this piece of crap out front in the garbage." Nearly blind with emotion and from the tears that were clouding his vision, he started for the front door. "This *never* happened. It's done, okay? It's all done."

He was almost at the entryway when he heard a noise come from Celeste that stopped him cold. An excruciating, mournful howl. He closed his eyes as a wave of nausea swept through him. A thud sounded as Celeste dropped to the floor and released another guttural moan. Somehow he managed not to vomit. Matt left the Flat Finn thing where it was by the door and went back into the kitchen.

Celeste lay in a heap on the floor, choking on her sobs.

"We can't have this in the house! It's not normal, Celeste. You're not doing this to us! You're not keeping that!" Matt had no idea how he was forming words right now. His thoughts were fuzzy, all rationale drowned out by the piercing ringing in his head. He cringed as she slammed her hands into the floor over and over.

He took a few steps toward her, and she lunged at him, pushing her fists into his chest as she tried to rush past him to reach Flat Finn. Matt chased her to the front door and reached out reflexively, grabbing her around the waist, pulling her back before she could touch the grotesque cardboard cutout. "Forget it. Consider it gone. This is over."

"Matty!" she screamed through sobs. "Just this one thing! Let me have him!"

"Absolutely not! Are you kidding me with this?"

"STAY AWAY FROM ME! HE BELONGS TO ME, NOT TO YOU! I GET TO HAVE THIS. MATT! I GET TO HAVE THIS! I DO!"

Matt froze, but kept her in his grasp. He had never heard her like this before. "Celeste...." His voice was softer now. From his own grief. From his own fear.

She spun around and fell into him, hitting his arms hard and still screaming. "YOU HAVE TO LET ME! YOU HAVE TO LET ME! I cannot do this without him! I cannot! I cannot! You must let me have him!" Her knees began to give out, and Matt lowered her to the ground, cradling her while she cried. He could feel her struggling to breathe. "I need to feel better. Help me, Matty. Please."

Matt held her tightly while he tried to pull himself together. "Okay. It's okay. Everything will be fine. You'll keep Flat Finn." Her breathing eased. "You'll keep him."

They stayed on the floor together as Celeste recovered. As they both recovered. She lay down, using his lap as a pillow, and Matt wiped her face dry with his hands.

Matt was too scared to say anything else, but finally she looked over at Flat Finn, towering above them, and spoke. "I know that your initial assessment of him is not exactly stupendous, but I truly believe that he is going to find a place in your heart. He means a great deal to me. I have missed Finn so profoundly, and it is reassuring to have him back."

"Honey," Matt started. "That's not...."

"I am fully aware that is not the real Finn. He is a placeholder. Like when a child has a favorite blanket, Flat Finn will be my security object. Only with more character than an unhygienic, unattractive, dirty fabric scrap."

Matt just nodded.

"I want to talk about Finn right now," she said.

"Okay." He paused. "Let's talk about Finn."

"Where do you think that Finn would be now? He was going to travel, remember? Mom and Dad were going to be furious, correct? They would not have been pleased that he was going to spend a full year exploring the world instead of studying at college, but I think that it would have been thoroughly fascinating. Do you remember what he planned for this adventure?"

"I do."

"If I were to hazard a guess, I would say that Finn would quite likely be in Portugal right now."

Matt took her hand in his. "And what would he be doing there?"

"A strenuous bike tour through indescribably beautiful landscapes." She shut her eyes. "Where would he go next?"

"After he'd romanced all the available women?"

Celeste laughed softly. "Yes."

"Finland, of course."

"He would not! You are very funny, but that location was not on his list."

"Fine. Then he would go to the Netherlands."

"And next winter he would ski in Austria. I know that would be a favorite of his. Can we go online later and look at pictures?"

"Sure. That would be fun."

Celeste rolled onto her side, letting him rub her back. "Tell me more, Matty. Tell me about all the adventures that Finn would have. I like how you describe things. Can you do that for me?"

Matt smiled. "I can do that. Sure. I'll do whatever you need." He took a deep breath. "Well, Mali has a number of volunteer opportunities...."

Staying

Flat-Out Love, Chapter 8,
Matt's Point of View (MPOV)

Matt Watkins This status update is way too condescending. That means it's talking down to you, you may not have known that.

Finn is God Ugh. Is there a shorter word that means "uncooperative" and can be spelled with letters cut out from an assortment of magazines? Getting really tired here.

Julie Seagle Everything should be open 24 hours a day, all the time. I can't be expected to know in advance when I'm going to need anything.

Matt took his time walking home. Even though he had a ton of work to do that night, even though his messenger bag was now cutting deeply into his shoulder after the T was delayed, and even though he was starving and desperately wanted to scrounge for food, he wasn't eager to get home. She was there. Julie. The girl who had invaded their family and disrupted the delicate balance Matt had fought so hard to establish.

Her presence here was a reminder of everything Matt had lost. They were all lying about Finn again, the way they always did to those who didn't already know. *He's off traveling, that wild boy! Such an adventurer and humanitarian!* It was really disgusting. If it weren't for Celeste's fragile state, Matt wouldn't put up with this, much less actively participate. Julie being here made their dysfunction all the more pronounced. The way she responded to Flat Finn's presence was so kind—and Julie was so smart—that it was certain she must look at them all with utter dismay. What made it all worse was that she had an appeal that tugged at a distant part of him, although he was fully aware she would never look at him with any hint of a romantic overtone. That was just a fact. Maybe a few years ago it could have been different, because Matt had been different, but certainly not now. Nor did it really matter because Matt didn't have the desire, nor the capability, for anything outside of what he was already dealing with. Julie would be gone in a few days, and they could go back to hiding out in their controlled, insulated world.

As much as having her around threatened the equilibrium of the household, Matt would miss Julie. That didn't make sense, considering he'd only known her for a few days, but he couldn't deny that she had an energy and light about her that brought Celeste noticeable happiness. No, perhaps not happiness, exactly. But he saw a spark in Celeste that he hadn't seen in a long time. Watching the two of them on the couch the other night while they went through Julie's course book and photos on her computer terrified him, but he also saw Celeste press Julie for interaction in a rather wonderful way. His terror had more to do with how Julie was going to respond to this kid who carted around a cardboard brother. The truth was that Julie's ability to navigate so seamlessly around the Flat Finn issue ticked him off. How she was able to relate so well to Celeste (well, and to Flat Finn) seemed profoundly unfair after Matt had done everything that he could for his sister with minimal progress. Plus, it was plain embarrassing. What Julie must think of them all ....

He shook his head, trying to clear his thoughts as he walked up the steps to the gray house just off Brattle Street in Cambridge. It was impossible to come home and not have a moment of pain. There would always be the split second of anticipation that Finn would be there. That he might come bounding down the stairs to tackle Matt in a spontaneous wrestling match, or that his music might be blasting so loudly from his room that the entire house would tremble from the booming bass. Matt would probably never get over it, but each day he had a touch of happiness in that moment of blind hope. He shook his head again.

He was edgy tonight, too, because it was impossible not to worry about what had gone on while he'd been at school today. Julie was an unknown factor that had played into Celeste's day. Even Julie's reassurances over the phone that Celeste was fine hadn't comforted him much, because he didn't like anyone else being involved. And saying that things were "fine" just had to be inaccurate. Things were never "fine" with Celeste. Even if picking up Celeste from school hadn't been an outright disaster, something unusual, or strained, or difficult must have taken place. Julie had no long-term experience with Celeste, and just because Julie had done well with his sister over the matter of a few days didn't mean that she knew what to say. And what not to say. It wouldn't take much to push Celeste over the edge, and for all Matt knew, he was walking into a house now filled with a hundred Flat

Finns. A Flat Army poised to defend and protect Celeste.

Matt would grab whatever leftovers he could find in the fridge and duck up to his room. He had a long night of schoolwork ahead of him.

It was immediately obvious when he stepped into the house that something was off, but he couldn't quite narrow down what that something was. He could feel the tension in his shoulders increase as he walked into the kitchen, and he felt as though all of his senses were malfunctioning.

Julie turned to him and smiled. Without meeting her eyes, Matt set his messenger bag on one of the stools by the breakfast counter. He looked at the plate in front of him.

"What is this?"

"It's a gastronomical representation of *Cat on a Hot Tin Roof*." Julie put her hands on her hips. Her dark hair was in a loose ponytail, and she had on rolled-up jeans and a light, flowy top. "Don't you see it?" she continued. "The clear depiction of the struggle for sexual identity as evidenced by the two phallic shapes?"

Matt stared at her. This girl was confusing. "What are you talking about?"

"What are *you* talking about? It's manicotti, you nut. What do you think it is?"

"I know *that*." Even though Julie had just used the words *sexual* and *phallic*, he still had brain function, for God's sake. "I was referencing the noticeable absence of takeout cartons. You made dinner?"

"Celeste and I made dinner," Julie corrected him.

"And they did a wonderful job." His mother appeared and placed her wine glass on the counter.

Matt briefly registered that Erin was drinking, but the lure of the food in front of him dulled any concern he had about that. He immediately sat down and started eating, barely hearing his mother as she talked to Julie. An actual home-cooked dinner? And ... Celeste helped do this? This was entirely weird. But, God, did it taste good. Matt didn't normally care for manicotti, but this dinner seemed like the best thing he'd ever eaten.

Someone had cooked for him. What a stupid thing to think. Or to care about.

"You're home late. How was school? Did your meeting go well?" Erin asked.

Matt nodded and wiped his mouth with a napkin. A cloth napkin, at that. "Very good. Sorry I'm home late. And even sorrier that I've managed to double my workload by agreeing to be a research assistant." This was also adding to Matt's stress level. He would potentially be spending more time at school and therefore be less available to Celeste. Finding a way to make this work was going to be difficult.

"This is with Professor Saunders, correct? He has an excellent reputation, so this is an important opportunity for you." Erin took a sip of her wine, and Matt looked away. "You'll have to be incredibly diligent with your work."

"I realize that." Like he needed reminding about anything related to his academics. It wasn't as though Matt had a long history of completely screwing up in school—he'd gotten into MIT, after all—yet his mother frequently implied that his education was somehow perilously hanging in the balance, and he might just crash off the academia scale at any given moment. "In fact," Matt said as he stood up, "I should get upstairs and get to work. I'll finish dinner up there. Thanks, Julie." He took his bag and plate and started out of the kitchen. It had been a long day, and the last thing he needed was to be around Erin and her air of doubt around his competence. He stopped at the doorway. "Julie?"

"Yeah?"

"So things went all right today?" Asking her to pick up Celeste today had taken every ounce of nerve he had. But once—just once—he hadn't wanted to drop what he was doing to attend to his sister. But he felt awful about it, as though he had let down Celeste yet again. Meeting with his professor had been important to him, because as much as he loathed the way his mother rode him constantly about his education, she hadn't managed to kill his insatiable interest in learning. He'd delayed a year of school after Finn died. Wasn't that enough to let him off the hook for asking Julie for help today? No, it wasn't really. One day could change everything. He knew that all too well.

"Totally fine. I told you that when you called. Both times," she said.

He admired the tone in her voice, the same one that she used a number of times the day they went apartment hunting. It actually was a bit Finn of her. She wasn't being mean or making fun of him, but she could get away with slightly teasing him without making him feel bad. The way that she treated him like... well, like a normal person... was slightly jarring. Nice, but jarring in its familiarity. And he was both grateful and anxious from the lack of detail that she offered about the pickup.

"Okay. Thanks again."

When he reached his room, he shut the door, opened his laptop and finished his dinner. He browsed a few of the message boards that he frequented and tried to focus on fine-tuning his attack on another user's take on internet security. Matt loved internet security issues, but tonight his concentration was shaky. Eventually he caved to what he really wanted to do, which was check an e-mail account that he used on occasion, the one that the he used to write Celeste so that she could pretend to get e-mails from Finn. It was part of a fantasy world that she liked to maintain, a world in which Finn was still alive and sending her updates on his travels. Yes, it was a little crazy, but Matt knew that Celeste understood it was essentially a game. She knew it wasn't real. Even Matt had to admit that there were moments when he didn't mind concocting stories and tweaking pictures. He'd even made that Facebook page under "Finn is God" because he knew that Celeste would then sit with him on occasion and browse through photos and silly status updates. All this Finn stuff often seemed to be the only thing that drew Celeste into him. Or drew anyone into him, maybe.

Of course, he hadn't planned on Julie sending Finn is God a friend request on Facebook. Or writing to him. It was so incredibly stupid to have replied to that first message when she let him know that she was staying in his room for a few days, but... hell, Matt just hadn't been thinking. And the lie had already been set up, so he'd just gone with it. What was the alternative? Write her back and say, *Actually, Julie, this isn't Finn. It's Matt, across the hall. Sorry, but Finn is dead, and my mother gave me a sharp one-liner*

about how we were all going to stick with Celeste's
preferred version of events just to make things easier,
and that was that. No hard feelings? If Matt were
honest with himself, he'd allow that it had been
surprisingly nice to hide behind that degree of
anonymity when he wrote her back. Julie would
never *meet* this fictional Finn, so what did it really
matter anyway? It wasn't as if she would be around
for very long. *Nobody* was around for very long
because then they couldn't all act like lunatics by
letting Celeste pretend that Finn was alive and well
and cleaning up elephant dung in Africa or whatnot.

A few more days and an apartment would
probably turn up. True, Matt and Julie's day of
hunting the Boston/Cambridge area for something
non-cockroach and/or hooker-infested didn't go well,
and this was a horrible time to try to find a place to
live, but Matt had no doubt that Julie would be gone
by the weekend.

And then life would go back to normal. Whatever
that meant around here.

He really couldn't figure out Julie. She looked so
relaxed, so disarmingly at home here, and so totally
unfettered by life's challenges. Like that first moment
he'd seen her outside her nonexistent apartment. She
could have been miserable and upset, but she was
still talkative and ... so very *her*. Even in crummy
circumstances. Matt was momentarily unnerved
when she'd virtually collapsed into him on the
escalator the other day, because not only was she
genuinely panicked, but.... Well, it had been a long
time since he'd had real physical contact with
someone. Not that he was a particularly affection-
seeking guy, but his parents and sister certainly

didn't look for opportunities to hug him, and he hadn't been on a date since Ellen broke up with him. Holding Julie in his arms and keeping her from dropping to the floor was the first time that he'd been that physically close to someone in years. But the point was that she bounced back from the incident incredibly well. And the way that she'd managed that first dinner with Flat Finn? Matt didn't know what to think about that. She was fun, and Matt didn't really know what to do with *fun* these days. It was rather ironic that Julie seemed so at ease in this house full of deeply uneasy people.

He sighed and leaned back in his chair, annoyed at his level of distractedness. Changes in the household were not going to be good for his studies.

Julie's voice echoed softly outside his door. Matt tipped his head and listened, biting his lip to stop the smile that threatened to form. She was talking to Flat Finn. "You and I will be spending more time together, so I expect continued model behavior. Deal? You're thinking about it? Let me know. Excuse me while I go to your namesake's room and unpack. We'll talk later." She was... a funny girl.

Matt took a thick textbook from his bag. Just as he got comfortable sitting on his bed with his back against a pillow, Erin knocked and simultaneously opened the door.

"Matthew?" She stepped into the room and closed the door behind her. "I thought you should know that Julie is staying with us."

Matt continued reading, but murmured. "I know. She hasn't found an apartment yet."

"No. I mean that Julie will be staying with us for good. I asked her to stay."

Matt slammed the book shut and glared at Erin. "You did what? What do you mean *for good*?"

Erin crossed her arms. "I asked her to stay. She can help out with Celeste. Your father is leaving on his trip soon, and we could use someone else around here."

Right, because their father was such a massive help when it came to Celeste?

"You've got to be kidding me? We can't have her in the house! Why would you do this?"

"Matthew, lower your voice," Erin said in an angry whisper.

He stood up and moved to stand next to his mother. "How in the hell are we supposed to make this work?"

"Calm down. I don't see what the problem is. Julie will pick up Celeste from school and be with her until someone else gets home in the evenings. Your afternoons are now free, and considering the workload you have this year, I should think you'd be pleased. It's a perfect solution."

The room seemed be spinning. His mother had to be out of her mind. "And just what are we supposed to do about Finn, huh?"

"Finn?"

"Yes. My dead brother," Matthew spat out under his breath. "My brother who Julie thinks is—"

"Matthew!" Erin's face froze and it took a moment for her to speak again. "There is no reason to tell Julie about our personal business. The point is that this is a smooth solution."

"Oh, Mom... Please don't do this."

"This is not a discussion. I'm simply telling you about the arrangements that have been made. And, goodness, you need to relax. There's really no reason to get to riled up." Erin frowned and tucked her hair behind her ear. "I'm going into my office to get some work done. Make sure Celeste has her lights off by eight-thirty, okay?"

Once alone, Matt dropped to the bed and lay on his side. He closed his eyes for a minute. The sound of the shower running in the next room soothed him a bit. He couldn't even process what his mother had done. Perhaps there was no point in trying because there was nothing to be done about it. The decision had been made, as most decisions were in this house, without any regard for how it would affect him. It wasn't that shocking. The systems and routines that he'd worked so hard to put in place and maintain for Celeste's benefit could easily come undone now.

He opened his eyes and found himself staring at the thick wooden leg of his desk. Of course, it wasn't *his* desk. This wasn't *his* room. It was Finn's. Matt's real room, the one that been his when life was happier, was across the hall and being taken over by a stranger who liked Flat People, Coolattas, and "interesting."

Things were about to get really interesting.

Matt squinted at the desk leg and then rolled off the bed until he was sitting on the floor. Huh. He'd never noticed this before, and he took a moment before crawling forward a few feet, nearly entranced by what he was seeing. He knelt down and touched his hand to the old wood, feeling the letters that had been carved there so many years ago.

Are you ready to jump?

His computer sounded and Matt slowly got to his chair, suddenly much more at peace with the swirl of

changes that seemed to be engulfing him. He clicked
the trackpad a few times.

> Dear Finn—
> Hope you don't mind if I hang in your
> room for a little longer. Your mom
> suggested I ditch the impossible idea of
> trying to find a Boston apt. and stay here.
> Mornings at college, afternoons with
> Celeste, and evenings defending your
> room against monsters.
> Being a girl and all, I'm resisting the urge
> to immediately paint your bedroom pink
> and plaster the wall with pictures of
> unicorns and rainbows. No promises on
> how long I can hold out.
> How is South Africa? Celeste is waiting for
> pictures... Hint, hint.
> —Julie

He smiled softly. If Julie could actually defend his
current room against the multitude of monsters that
had taken up residence there after Finn's death, she'd
really be one tough girl. If she could make those go
away, then.... God, if only. Her enthusiasm, her
optimism, her hope? They were all so far from where
he was.

He read her message again. And then he sat
quietly and stared at the screen.

He should end this now. He knew that.

But then what? Then she would leave, as anyone
would, because nobody would stay after learning the
truth. While Matt was—if he was honest—a bit taken
aback at how well Julie and Celeste connected, the
important thing was that Celeste was responding to
someone. She certainly hadn't to him, no matter how

hard he had tried. It would be understandable to let someone else try to bring his sister back, wouldn't it?

With the noise of the shower as his background, Matt began to type. Life wasn't often fun or relaxed anymore, but as he wrote to Julie, a levity swept over him. Even a touch of joy at being able to joke and talk freely with someone who didn't look at him as broken. Even as he told himself that Celeste was the one who needed Julie, there was a small part of him that wondered if he might need her, too. If he would ever be ready to jump.

Maybe, Finn, he whispered as he typed. *Probably not, but maybe.*

The Elevator

Flat-Out Love, Chapter 19, MPOV

Matt Watkins Today's Contrition Club meeting has been cancelled: words cannot express how deeply, deeply sorry we are.

Finn is God "It's a possibootily" is my favorite new phrase. I've decided it means, "You may or may not get laid later."

Julie Seagle If I'd known how many times I would hear "Celebration" in my lifetime, I would have murdered Kool and his whole Gang years ago.

Matt knew that Julie was with Seth tonight. He didn't know exactly what was going on with them—and not that it was any of his business—but he still didn't like it. The phone call that he accidentally heard yesterday bothered him more than he wanted to admit. What had she said? *You mean you've had enough time with Celeste and me in the coffeehouse? You don't find that romantic, and sexy, and hot?* And now she was going out with him tonight. Or worse, not going out, but staying in. She'd said something about him making her dinner at his apartment. He didn't know anything about this Seth kid, and for all anybody knew, Julie's date had a long history of violent criminal behavior. She left with the car only fifteen minutes ago, but Matt was already edgy. His fingers tapped rhythmically across his desk and he stared at his laptop's screen. He didn't know where Seth lived, but he wasn't crazy about the idea of Julie driving around Boston by herself at night. She might have to park far away and walk down unlit back streets.

Matt pushed his chair back and walked to Celeste's room. Her door was cracked open, so he knocked as he entered the room. His sister was on the bed, laying flat on her back, with both arms extended straight up and holding a thesaurus.

"Oh, Matthew, I am delighted that you chose this moment to stop by this evening. I have a project for school that Julie has been assisting me with, and I was hoping to work with her. Do you know when she will return?"

"Oh. I don't know. After you're asleep, I imagine."

"So then you do believe that Julie will be returning back here tonight? I had wondered if perhaps this was going to be an overnight excursion, in which case I was unsure about what time to expect her tomorrow."

"Celeste!"

"Why are you exhibiting a reaction that involves such a chastising tone? I understand that Julie is of an age where one may possibly engage in certain activities that often are conducted only in late hours, during which—"

"Stop right there, please." Matt held up both hands. "We are not having this conversation or even thinking about this subject matter. Is that clear?"

"*You* may not be thinking about this subject matter, but as it directly affects my school project, I am."

Matt sighed. He looked to the bay windows off to his left. It was dark out, indeed. Certain things were more likely to happen at night. Again, not that it was his business, but there were safety issues to consider.

Maybe he could give Julie one of those handheld alarms. Or pepper spray. It was probably a good idea. He glanced at Flat Finn, who was positioned in one corner of the room, facing the wall. "What is Flat Finn doing? If he's urinating on the floor, you're cleaning it up."

"Matthew! Flat Finn is most certainly not urinating. Do not be so outlandish."

"Is he in trouble? He has to stand in the corner and think about what he's done?"

Celeste lowered her book. "No. I was finding him disruptive."

"Seriously? How exactly was he disruptive? Were his hinges squeaking?"

"I felt as though he were looming over me tonight. On occasion, I need a bit of distance. It was Julie's suggestion that there may be times I find I do better with a break from him. So tonight we are having a break. I am entitled to some privacy, Julie pointed out."

"Oh." Matt shifted his weight. "I think that's a valid point."

"Did you want to speak to me about something in particular? I need to get back to my compilation of alternate words and concepts."

"I... I... " Matt suddenly felt mildly embarrassed.

Celeste blinked at him. "Yes?"

"I was just wondering if you knew this Seth guy's last name?"

"I do not. We could call Julie and find out right now if you need immediate satisfaction."

"No, no. We don't need to do that."

"Why are you interested in his last name? Are you developing a surname fixation? I have always found surnames to be quite interesting myself, so when you find out, please let me know, and I will likely be able to tell you quite a bit about—"

"What? No, no, I'm not interested in surnames. Forget it." Matt turned to the door.

"Oh, I understand!" Celeste said, suddenly excited. "You would like to investigate Julie's romantic interest! An amateur background check of sorts!"

Matt didn't say anything.

"I am right! You are experiencing profound jealousy!"

He turned back her way. "No, I am not *experiencing profound jealousy*. Don't be ridiculous. I just think that as her... local family, or whatever... we should be aware of who she is spending time with. There are safety issues here. She is out at night with a stranger."

Celeste beamed. "I can see that in fact you most definitely *are* thinking about the aforementioned subject matter from which you steered me away. You have concerns that she may be becoming intimate with—"

"Celeste, seriously, knock it off." Matt glared at her. "Forget I asked anything."

"Unfortunately, I do not know Seth's last name, but I know him from the many visits that Julie and I have taken to the cafe where he works. I have done an investigation of my own on this local student and part-time barista, and I have found nothing indicative of sociopathology. There is no reason for us not to hold him in high regard."

"Okay. That's good," Matt said.

"There is, however, one concerning factor," Celeste said slowly.

"What? What's wrong with him?"

"What I dislike quite strongly about Seth is that he currently has the romantic, and possibly sexual, attention of the young woman with whom you are finding yourself progressively more and more besotted."

Matt practically snorted. "Oh, God. Good night, Celeste. Perhaps a good night's sleep will bring you to your senses."

"Perhaps a good night's sleep will bring *you* to your senses!" Celeste said matter-of-factly as she lay down and again lifted the heavy thesaurus. "A good night's repose. A good night's slumber. A good night's...."

Matt shut her door and went back to his room. Celeste was out of her mind in more ways than one. He was not *besotted* with anyone. He took his laptop, sat up in bed to work, and cranked the music with a remote. *Besotted.* What a ridiculous word.

He checked his e-mail and found a message from Julie telling Finn that Celeste loved her barrette. And that she was exhausted from being up so late the night before. Matt smiled softly. Yes, it had been about three a.m. when he'd finally shut down the computer. He couldn't believe how long they talked. Her message also said that she would look for him on chat later tonight. Meaning, Matt noted, that she was planning on coming home. The posing-as-Finn thing was a little awkward, obviously, but he and Julie seemed to have found a comfortable online friendship that worked for them both. It really wasn't much different than the other online communications he had. Or not *entirely* different. But it wasn't as though Julie told Finn everything, either. She had never mentioned Seth at all.

Matt sent a quick Finn reply, knowing full well that Julie was probably not checking out e-mails while on a date.

Yet a minute later, a chat message from Julie popped up.

> **Julie Seagle** Am flipping stuck in an elevator. Alone. Miserable. Help is on the way supposedly, but I am not enjoying this experience. Starting to seriously panic. Sweating, shakes, visions of brutal death.

This wasn't good. Julie could not be in good shape. Matt had seen what the escalator ride had done to her, and the idea that she was dangling in a steel box however many stories up was probably not going over well. And there was no one there to catch her this time. A little humor seemed in order.

> **Finn is God** What??? Oh, no! Do not panic. Have you forgotten that I am a superhero?

> **Julie Seagle** I had forgotten! Feel totally safe now. Okay, you fly under the elevator and lift me up to safety. Ready? Go!

> **Finn is God** Unfortunately my flying powers were deactivated because I abused my superhero status. Apologies. I have other powers, though, that will get you through this.

> **Julie Seagle** Give it your best shot.
> Convince me that I'm not a million feet in
> the air.

Matt thought back to the first time that he stood at the edge of an open door as an airplane held him thousands of feet in the air, poised above certain death. Terror didn't quite capture it. The safety of his training and the emergency backup chute did little to reassure him. There were a few minutes when Matt was so frozen with fear that he couldn't even back out of jumping. Yet he wanted to jump more than anything. And Finn was there, so high on what they were about to do, so revved up with an energy and fearlessness that Matt wanted desperately for himself. Denial was impossible in those circumstances, so he took another approach. One that might help Julie now.

> **Finn is God** You can't pretend you are
> not up high, because you are.

> **Julie Seagle** These are delightful powers
> you have. Thank you so much. I feel a
> million times better.

> **Finn is God** Accept that you're up high
> and embrace it. Take control. It's like
> when I go skydiving. I don't actually love
> heights. It scares the hell out of me to be
> in that plane, looking down at the ground.
> But I jump through that fear and turn it into
> euphoria.

> **Julie Seagle** I would never in a million
> years go skydiving.

Matt hesitated before typing.

> **Finn is God** What if I took you?

> **Julie Seagle** I'd still be jumping out of a plane alone, just like I'm alone in this stupid elevator.

> **Finn is God** You wouldn't be alone. I'd take you tandem, so you'd be strapped to me. We'd jump together.

> **Julie Seagle** How would that work?

Now that he had raised this idea, he realized describing it might carry a certain connotation that may not go over well. A risky connotation. But it wasn't Matt's fault. It's not as though he invented tandem skydiving so that he would one day be able describe it to a girl stuck in a broken elevator.

> **Finn is God** You'd be in front of me, your back pressed into my chest.

He waited. Matt looked away from the screen for a minute, listening to the music that was filling his room. Out of the corner of his eye, he saw the image on the screen move.

> **Julie Seagle** That part doesn't sound so awful.

The tension that he was holding rushed from his body.

> **Finn is God** No. It doesn't sound so awful, does it?

Julie Seagle So then tell me more.

Finn is God Okay. Pretend we're going right now. Ready?

Julie Seagle Ready.

Finn is God We're in the plane, and it's loud and cold. You see duct tape over parts of the interior of the plane and wonder if jumping is the worst idea you've ever had, but I tell you you'll be fine. We both have on the full skydiving suits, helmets, goggles, chutes. The suit is tight, and it gives you the illusion of being safe, secure. You're full of mixed emotions. Pride, anxiety, exuberance, terror.

Julie Seagle Nausea?

Matt smiled. Even when Julie was scared, she was cute.

Finn is God That's not an emotion! But, yes, nausea.

Julie Seagle Then what?

Matt had started this without thinking, and without understanding what he was doing, but she was responding. So the only thing to do was continue.

Finn is God Your mind is racing. Did you remember to turn off the oven at home? Your car needs an oil change. You're out of shampoo. Why do washing machines eat socks? Do they taste good? Should you try eating socks? You wonder if you should back out, if this was a mistake. You didn't tell anyone that you were jumping today, and now what if you die? You worry that you'll forget what to do, that you won't remember when to pull the chute. I show you the altimeter. The plane is only halfway up to where we need to be, and it already feels so high. But you're not in any danger.

Julie Seagle Finn, I'm scared. The elevator is shaking.

Matt didn't like this. Elevators got jammed all the time, especially in older apartment buildings, which is likely where Seth lived. The elevator was probably shaking because the fire department was there banging around, and he bet that the vibrations and the metallic noise were increasing Julie's panic, but that she was not actually in any true danger. Rational thinking, however, wasn't erasing his concern for how she must be feeling. He wanted her to feel safe.

Finn is God I know you are, but I've got you. You're not in the elevator. You're with me. I stand you up and try to push your body away from mine, reminding you that you are tightly strapped to me and that I won't let anything happen. It's my job to control our jump and my job to pull the chute if you don't. You're safe. Tell me that you trust me.

Julie Seagle I trust you.

Matt took a deep breath. Something just happened between them. Julie felt something for him. She did. He could tell even through this online world.

Whether it was him or Finn didn't really matter. It was a difference of names really, that's all. Yes, he had never volunteered in Africa or scuba dived in remote locations in search of rare coral, but Matt used to have a good dose of Finn's adventurous spirit. So the essence of his communication as Finn was real and it was what had connected them online. And Julie needed that relationship they'd been building, the one that had crept up without warning. She needed him to talk her through this. And so he would.

> **Finn is God** We're high enough now, and one of the instructors opens the door, sending a powerful rush of air into the cabin. Your heart nearly stops when I start to walk you to the edge. As much as you're terrified, you're also starting to feel the rush, the thrill you get from being on the brink.

Matt ran both hands through his hair and bit his lip. God, what was he doing? She was his friend. They were *just* friends, right?

> **Finn is God** We're at 15,000 feet now, and when you look down at the ground, you immediately try to step away from the door. You want to bail on this. I back you up, and we let someone else jump first. I put my arms around your waist and pull you in, holding you, letting you know I'm with you. I tell you that you can do this, that you're strong enough and brave enough. I tell you that you can do anything. So you nod and agree to jump.
>
> We move to the edge of the plane again and pause. You cross your arms over

> your chest and lean your head back into
> me like I told you. I start to rock us back
> and forth, getting us ready to jump. And
> then we go.

Matt knew that he might have gone too far. That he might lose her now.

Or that Finn might lose her.

But he couldn't stop because the thought of being able to hold her, to feel her against him while his arms wrapped around her protectively....

It was suddenly heartachingly clear how much he wanted this and how easy it was to imagine it with near provocative clarity. She was not just his friend. She was more.

Matt had spent quite a bit of time, he realized, watching Julie. Not just how beautiful she was, but how she moved, how she spoke, what made her laugh. He knew almost too much. The way her body eased past his in the narrow kitchen, the way she brushed her hair from her face when she was studying, the way her eyes narrowed when she disagreed with something in a textbook. He knew her determination, her warmth, her openness.

Celeste was right. Damn it.

Matt's breathing picked up a bit when she replied. She wanted him to keep going.

> **Julie Seagle** How do I feel when we
> jump?

> **Finn is God** The minute we hit the air,
> you are surprisingly relaxed. All of your
> problems seem to go away. Your stomach
> doesn't drop. There's no falling sensation.
> It's just freeing. It's as close to flying as

you'll ever get. A calm like you've never
known before, and you don't want it to
end.

Matt put a hand on the back of his neck. God, was
he sweating?

Finn is God So we freefall like this for
5,000 feet. We don't want it to stop. We
want to feel like this forever, lost in this
experience. This is why people pull their
chutes late, because freefalling is like a
drug.

Julie Seagle Or something else, I'm
guessing.

Finn is God Yes, or something else. They
do call it an "airgasm" for a reason.

Julie Seagle I can see why. But we have
to pull the chute.

Finn is God Yes, we have to pull the
chute. So I do it. And it jerks us back—
hard—but then we're falling smoothly,
softer than before, easily. We're drifting
together. It's quieter now, and you can
hear my voice.

Julie was completely with him, he knew. She was
as much out of that elevator and in the heart of this
fabricated but still very real moment as Matt was.

Julie Seagle And what do you say to me?

Matt thought. What did he want to say to her?
That right now he was accepting that it drove him
crazy when she sat so close to him when they studied

together, especially on his bed? That, while of course she was always beautiful, his legs would nearly give out when she came downstairs in the morning with her hair thrown into a messy knot smack on the top of her head and her robe wrinkled and barely tied? That he knew she liked to get dressed up for her nights out, but that he liked her Saturday afternoon look of yoga pants and no makeup? That the way she cared for Celeste with such abandon and acceptance moved him more than he could fathom? That she was skilled and talented and warm and patient enough that, seemingly without even trying, she'd drawn him in from the cold world where he had been living since that horrible day when Finn died?

Did he want to tell her the truth? Maybe she knew already or maybe it wouldn't matter. All the hours of writing back and forth over the past few months might have added up to something that could go beyond this virtual relationship. And that's what they were doing, whether either of them could really admit it; they were having a relationship. More specifically, they were having two relationships. The blending of those two, that was what could make this all fall apart. *Would* make it fall apart, Matt realized.

As Finn, he had fallen into an online relationship that was safe and controlled. He could show Julie sides of him that he wanted to and guard the others. He could show her who he wanted to be.

As Matt, their friendship had to battle all the real-world challenges that he carried with him, and he had no clue how to act like any guy Julie would take interest in. He didn't know how to flirt anymore, and half the time that he was around her Matt was stressed to no end about what Julie was going to do next with Celeste, or whether she would somehow find out about the family's lies. And while he didn't really care much about how he looked, he figured that a girl as breathtaking as he found Julie to be could easily attract modelesque guys. On the other hand, she didn't seem like someone who would date just for looks. She was too smart and dynamic to be that superficial. Maybe that was the problem. She was everything that Matt wasn't. Not anymore. She was so well rounded that it nearly hurt to be around her. As things were, while they had established a friendship and a certain companionship, she wasn't falling for him. She was falling for Finn, a part of Matt that no longer fit into the real world.

> **Julie Seagle** Shit. The elevator is working now.

> **Finn is God** That's good news!

> **Julie Seagle** Right now it doesn't feel like it. I'll find you later.

Matt shut his laptop. What the hell had just happened to him? To *them*? He got up and went down to the kitchen. He needed water. And probably a cold shower. Or two. He was definitely more riled up than he'd been in a very long time.

He stood at the same counter where Julie grilled him about Celeste after her first dinner here. She'd been relentless in her questions about Flat Finn, but not once did she seem put off. A bit pushy, perhaps, but always very kind. She just wanted to understand, and who could blame her? Matt hopped up and sat on the counter in Julie's spot and downed a tall glass of ice water.

What was he going to do?

Maybe nothing. He might as well try to enjoy this online relationship for as long as he could. At some point it would probably fade out the way most things do anyway. Julie was presumably with Seth right now, so it's not as if that thinly veiled elevator chat had caused her to brush aside her evening date.

No, he told himself. *This was wrong. Julie deserves the truth. She hasn't done anything wrong, she didn't ask for this.*

So he would tell her. Tonight when she got home, he would tell her everything, and he would deal with the fallout. That elevator chat between them had gone too far, and he had to put a stop to this. It was clear to him that this was the only choice. He'd dealt with everything falling apart before, and he would do it again.

There. It was decided, and the torturous back and forth debate about what to do was over.

He shut off most of the downstairs lights, but made sure to leave the front porch light on. He got to the top of the stairs before he came back down and also turned on the entryway light and one in the living room before going back up. He stopped at the top of the stairs. The light was on in his parents' room, and he could see Erin standing in the middle of the room with a full wine glass in her hand. She really shouldn't be drinking, and he could tell by the slight sway in her stance that she had already had more than enough.

"Mom." Matt stood just outside her room. "What are you doing?"

"What is it, Matthew?" Erin didn't bother to look his way, but kept her eyes glued to the view of the street through the window.

He stepped closer and moved in front of her. "Mom." He could see that her eyes were slightly puffy.

"Hi, honey." She sniffed. "Is everything okay?"

While he hated her drinking, it was the one thing that seemed to make Erin at all motherly. "Yeah, everything is fine. Where's Dad? What are you doing?"

"Roger is up on the third floor in the guest room. He's got that dreadful cold that's been making him snore." She took a long drink from her glass. "I was just looking out at the snow. The streets haven't been plowed well, have they? It looks icy."

"They're okay, Mom."

"Maybe not. People shouldn't be driving tonight." She paused and Matt could see her hold on the wine glass tighten. Gently, he took the stem of the glass in one hand and peeled her fingers from the globe.

"The streets aren't bad at all. It just looks like it from here."

"Julie is out with the car, isn't she?" Erin looked directly at Matt. "Oh, have you heard from her? Oh, no, Matthew." Her eyes filled with tears.

"She's just fine. I promise. Please don't worry."

"You won't let anything happen to her, will you?" Erin touched her hand to his cheek, a small smile coming through the haze of alcohol and pain. "She's quite special to you, to all of us, isn't she?"

Matt nodded, but he couldn't say anything. He felt near tears himself.

Erin leaned into him, wrapping her arms over his shoulder and rubbing his back. This was so unlike

Erin, that for a moment Matt just stood still, unsure what to do. Eventually he leaned in and rested his head on his mother's shoulder. His free arm moved to hug her back.

"You won't tell her, Matthew, will you? Julie? Not yet."

"Mom...."

"Please."

Matt sniffed. "This isn't fair to her."

"Things feel better with her here, though, don't they? Like this? She makes things easier. Don't take that away. I miss him still, and now it's easier." Her hold around him grew tighter and Matt's resolve began to weaken.

"We can't keep doing this," he said softly.

"Just for a while. Let her figure it out in her own time. When she's ready, when she sees, it will be okay. I really believe that." He felt his mother's tears dampen his shirt and her fingers dug into him as she held on. "Please, Matthew. I am *begging* you. Let it come out in its own time."

"Okay." He nodded against her. "Okay."

"Thank you." He felt her relax a bit.

"You can't drink, Mom. You know that. No more?"

"No more," she agreed. "After tonight, no more. The snow, this time of year.... It triggers me. I think that your father and I will go out of town for New Year's. You can stay with Celeste, right?"

Matt dropped his hand and eased back. "Sure. I guess so."

"I think that I'll take a bath now. Relax."

"That's a good idea." Matt walked to the door, discouraged. Resigned. He almost turned back, but he knew that there was little chance she would say something to make this better, to make him feel loved.

He took a deep breath and knocked on Celeste's door. "Hey. I came to say good night."

"Good night, Matty." Celeste smiled as he sat down on her bed. "I am exceptionally tired this evening. The print in my thesaurus is obnoxiously small and my eyes suffered significant strain."

"I hope that you and your strained eyes rest well." He reached to turn off the small light on her nightstand that was aimed directly at nearby Flat Finn. A spotlight on a star.

"Julie said that after she helps me with my project tomorrow that she will teach me to make bouillabaisse. I have some reservations about her chosen assortment of seafood, notably the calamari tentacles, but I have agreed to be brave."

Matt patted her hand. "You are very brave."

"Will you come with us to the seafood market?"

"Do you want me to?"

"Yes, very much."

"Then I will."

"You should get your rest, too. Matthew, you look unusually exhausted tonight. I saw the recipe, and it requires a multitude of complicated steps, particularly the aioli which is composed of nineteen ingredients. Your assistance will be crucial to our success."

"Understood. Sleep well."

"Would you please set Flat Finn outside my door tonight? I would like him there for the benefit of his protection, but I will also be maintaining necessary space."

"Sure thing." He turned off the Flat Finn spotlight and retrieved their cardboard brother. "Good night, Celeste."

Matt shut the door to his room and pulled off his shirt. He was most definitely exhausted and wanted nothing more than to fall sleep and end this day. However, he held his phone when he crawled into bed. Matt lay on his back and stared into the darkness for forty-five minutes. He heard the creak of the stairs as Julie came home, and then he put in his earphones to try and block out the noise in his head. Then his e-mail sounded.

> I think I'm falling for you.

Matt looked at the screen for a long time. "Julie," he whispered aloud. For a moment he debated about what to do. Then he sent his reply.

> Good. I think I'm falling for you too. Let's not pull this chute.

Under The Christmas Tree

Flat-Out Love, Chapter 21, MPOV

Matt Watkins This season always brings back warm memories of peeing in terror on Santa's lap. Warm, wet memories.

Finn is God This is the season I always mix up "mistletoe" and "cameltoe." Either way, I'm getting slapped.

Julie Seagle The only thing that stands between you and your dreams is the fact that they are all illegal, immoral, and disgusting. Dream on, you little pervert!

This was probably a stupid idea. He'd probably gotten everything wrong, and Julie would think this was incredibly dopey. Nonetheless, Matt continued lighting the candles on the Christmas tree. Even as tall as he was, Matt still needed to stand on a step stool to reach the top of the enormous tree that he'd picked out. It had been a nightmare trying to find candleholders that could be attached to the branches, but that's what Julie described in her Thanksgiving chat with Finn, and Matt wanted to give her the Christmas setup that would make her happy. As much as she seemed quite comfortable here, this was her first year away from home, and she must be missing the familiarity and routine of the holiday at her house in Ohio. California certainly couldn't be the same, although he was sure that she would have a good time with her father.

Matt flinched as he burned his finger on a flame. Julie said this whole candles-on-the-tree thing could be dangerous, and she was right. He stepped back and surveyed the room. Okay, maybe she would like it. All of the house lights were off downstairs, but between the hundreds of twinkle lights on the ceiling and the candles on the tree and the ones nesting in green garlands, the room glowed warmly on this dark December night.

His e-mail alert sounded, and Matt checked his laptop.

> Finn—
> Thinking about you. That's all.
> —Julie

Matt bit his lip. He was lucky that she'd been holed up in her room for so long, probably about to go to sleep, and that he'd been able to get this all done. But now that he had, he was feeling embarrassed. What was the point? All he was doing was adding to Julie's feelings for Finn. This love triangle had reached new heights, and as much as Matt loved geometry, this was not the sort of triangle he wanted anything to do with.

Yet it had become progressively easier to keep up his role as Finn. It was sick, he knew that, but.... He didn't know how to get out of it. She had to see what was going on, didn't she? On some level? She easily accepted that Finn couldn't call. Way too easily. She wanted to believe in him. That had to be it. It's why she never pushed harder for him to get to a phone. But half the time, Matt himself forgot that this online thing wasn't real, because they both got so totally caught up in the increasing number of e-mails and chats that it felt like nothing else mattered. The feelings they were having were real. The context of the charade allowed for that. Being able to feel what he did for Julie, even in private, was addictive.

He didn't want to have to give that up. Not yet.

He would do it, though, if he could. If there would be no repercussions for Celeste, and for Erin, he would give this up and let Julie hate him. As she probably should.

> Julie—
> I hope this message goes through. I keep falling off the network here. Thinking about you too and miss you. (Is that weird? How can I miss you? But I do.)
> I'm not going to make it to Boston this month. I'll explain later. I'm so sorry. I don't know what to say.
> Glad you're still awake because I have a surprise for you. I know it won't make up for my not being there, but it's all I could think to do:
> Go into the living room.
> —Finn

This was it. She would come downstairs and laugh. He felt rotten about the e-mail because he knew that he'd just broken her heart a little by telling her that Finn wouldn't be home this month, but he was hoping that this Christmas thing he set up would help. He just had to buy some more time until... until... well, he wasn't exactly sure. Matt didn't want her upset. He knew that there wasn't any chance in hell that she could shift her feelings for who she *thought* was Finn over to him. The way Matt behaved with her online was so different from the way he could bring himself to do in person. And he'd promised Erin.

Matt looked at the tree. It really was quite spectacular. Then he frowned. He'd missed two of the candles near the top, so he got on the step stool again to light them.

"It's beautiful."

Julie's voice startled him and he almost lost his balance. "God, Julie. You scared me to death!"

She laughed. "I'm sorry. I just got a message from Finn, and he told me to come down here." She walked forward and lightly touched one of the branches. "It looks amazing."

Matt lit the last candle and stepped down. "Don't blame me if the house catches fire. This is all Finn's idea. He said it would make you happy?"

"It does make me happy. You did all this for me? I mean, Finn asked you to do this?"

Matt stuck his hands in his pockets and looked at the ceiling of lights. "He sent me a list of instructions and included detailed threats of bodily harm if I didn't follow his demands to the letter. I think I got it all." Matt moved to the coffee table. He glanced at the laptop's screen and shut the lid, hiding his e-mails to and from Julie. That had been careless of him. Maybe he wanted to get caught? "Yes, okay. Now we're supposed to lie under the tree. *That* does not sound traditional, but he said you would understand?" Matt looked doubtfully at her. He didn't understand the appeal of this concept, but it sounded important to her.

"I do understand. Come on!" She grabbed Matt's hand and pulled him to the floor with her. "I do this every year. You'll like it."

"Finn owes me," he muttered as he followed Julie and lay on his back to slide under the lower branches. Right now he felt like an unwilling participant in someone else's scheme, and the touch of her hand made him edgy because it felt too good. "Ow! If I lose an eye for this, I expect a massively expensive Christmas present from you both to compensate me for my troubles. Like a bedazzled eye patch or something."

"You have to go slow, silly. Don't fling yourself into the tree. Ease your way underneath. There. See?"

Matt scooted himself under the tree next to Julie, and instantly he could feel the shift. In himself, in reality... maybe even between them. The rest of the room disappeared, and there was just the two of them alone beneath the dance of the candlelight. There was no outside world anymore, because under the tree they were shielded from everything. It was beautiful. Beautiful and terrifying.

Matt took a deep breath and tried to relax. "Actually, this is sort of...nice," he said.

She turned to him. "I've never done this with anyone before. It's always just me."

"Oh. I thought I was supposed to stay here and do whatever it is we're supposed to do under the tree. Do you want me to go?" Matt started to slide out.

"No, stay!" She stopped him. "I like the company."

Matt smiled. He was glad that she wanted him here. "Okay. So what do we do?"

"We think about profound things."

"Ah. Philosophical ponderings and questions? I'll go first. Prove to me that you are not a figment of my imagination."

"Very funny."

"Am I in a computer simulation? Does the door swing both ways? How can something come from nothing? How do you know a line is straight?"

"Matt, stop it!" Julie laughed.

He enjoyed hearing her laugh, and he wanted to do whatever he could to keep her smiling and happy. She was adorable, and silly, and above everything, she was his friend. "If animals wanted to be eaten, would it be okay? If time stopped then started again, would we even know about it? What happens when you get scared half to death twice? What is creationism? What is ethical?"

"*What* is driving me crazy?" Julie asked, still giggling.

"No, *who* is driving you crazy?" Matt corrected her, smiling. He needed that. "But fine. If you don't like my line of deep thinking, then you lead the way."

Julie paused. "Now it all seems silly and juvenile."

"Tell me anyway." He could get her to talk to him the way that she talked online to Finn. At least, he would try.

"It's just...well, every year I lie under the tree, and...I don't know. Assess my life. Get into a sort of dream state and see where my thoughts lead me."

Matt crossed his long legs and rested his hands on his stomach. "I understand what you mean." He did, too, although he'd forgotten. When he hiked with Finn, there were times that Matt would find a quiet spot, usually with a grand view of the landscape and seemingly endless sky, and he would sit alone, taking some time to himself. It was on one of these hikes that he decided to do everything that he could to get into MIT. It would be hard, he might not be successful, but it was a dream worth chasing. So he would take in whatever stunning location Finn had taken them to, and he would sit and dream, close his eyes and let the pure air and the sound of silence flush through him, taking his thoughts and dreams further. Matt turned his head and looked at Julie. She was beautiful. "Why don't you close your eyes?"

"You close your eyes too."

"Okay."

Julie looked at him and waited. "You go first."

"No, you go first."

"We'll do it at the same time. I don't want to lie here with you watching me. Ready? Three, two, one, go." Julie shut her eyes. "Now we wait and see what comes to us."

Matt couldn't help himself. He continued to look at her. He wanted so much to reach over and put his hand on her cheek, to turn her face to his, to run his finger over her lips. He could move in closer, ever so slowly, and touch his mouth to hers. Kissing Julie would be perfection, he knew.

If her feelings for him—for Finn—were real, the kiss would stop the world.

Julie turned her head to the side and opened her eyes, but Matt couldn't look away. "I told you not to watch me," she whispered.

"I couldn't help it," he whispered back.

He was quiet for a moment. The charge between them—it was the elevator chat all over again. When there was trust, and honesty, and salvation, and love. He felt it. "Julie?"

"Yeah, Matt?"

He took a breath before he spoke, before he would say what was going to change everything. "It's like we're free—"

"Oh my God!" Julie said, cutting him off. "I totally forgot to ask you."

"Um... Ask me what?" Matt's heart was pounding.

"My friend Dana wants you to call her."

How could he for one minute have thought that her heart was his? Stupid. It was utterly impossible. It was good thing that she'd stopped him from saying anything. Matt fought to fake his usual tone, fending off the tremble that wanted to take over. "That's not asking me anything."

"Stop correcting me. She wants to go out with you, you dork!"

"Oh." Matt groaned with more drama than necessary, but he needed a reason to turn his head away. Getting flustered was not something he was used to. Or liked. "I don't know about that."

"Matty, come on. You never go out!" Julie pleaded. "She's really cool. You'd like Dana."

"I'll think about it. How's that?" he offered. The last thing that he felt like talking about with Julie was taking out her friend. Good God, this was awful. Julie sounded so genuinely enthusiastic about the idea of him going out with someone else. She felt nothing for him, that was now clear. There was no Finn/Matt crossover. So that was that. And he would regroup quickly because he knew how to do that when necessary.

"Have you ever had a girlfriend?"

Matt turned back and wrinkled his face. Did she really think he was that inexperienced? Or that he was that undesirable? "Of course I've had a girlfriend. What kind of question is that?"

Julie shrugged. "I don't know. You never mention anyone."

"I will admit that the romantic area of my life has been slow recently. I simply don't have time to go out with anyone right now. You know what my schedule is like with school and with Celeste."

"So you haven't dated since...you know? Celeste. The Flat Finn stuff."

"Not much. I had a pretty serious girlfriend, but then..." Matt struggled for how to say what he wanted to without saying too much. "Things changed around here."

"With Celeste?"

Matt nodded.

She didn't say anything for a minute. "When something happened?"

Matt nodded again.

"I'm sorry," Julie said. "Because whatever it is, I can tell that you're dealing with it too. Maybe someday you'll want to tell me about it."

"Maybe someday," Matt agreed. He wasn't one for talking deeply about anything to do with Finn's death, ever. But knowing that he could, even in this peripheral way, felt surprisingly good. "And my girlfriend at the time wasn't interested in staying together. Not everyone can tolerate my life. This house."

"I love Celeste, but she's hurting you, isn't she?"

"Don't say that. I would sell my soul for my sister."

"I know you would." Julie spoke slowly, and Matt knew that she was choosing her words with particular care. "But you must be angry with Finn for leaving. For making whatever happened to Celeste worse."

"I am angry with Finn." This was true.

He was angry with Finn for dying, for being dumb and reckless enough to jump into a car driven by someone clearly in the middle of a mental breakdown.

He was angry with Finn for being heroic enough to sacrifice his life for his mother's. Whether or not that was Finn's intention didn't matter. That's how it felt.

He was angry with Finn for causing everyone's lives to completely crumble.

He was angry with Finn for leaving Matt with an unspeakable mess that he was incapable of cleaning up. And for leaving him alone with a crazy family that didn't have the ability to love him.

"He has a right to his life, Matt."

The irony of Julie's words hit him hard. "Believe me, I know he does."

"Do you two usually get along?"

This was a difficult question to answer. "We used to. And then...we didn't." Yes, he and Finn were best friends, but even best friendships carry their own set of troubles. Finn's all-around skill and success combined with his modesty made their relationship inherently uneven. Matt knew that he would never be as perfect as Finn, and the way that Finn stepped in to care for Celeste after their mother's severe depression surfaced was more than Matt was able to do. Finn was better. At everything. With everybody. "Mostly because of the issues with my mother. He was always the hero. That wasn't easy for me, I guess."

"Celeste thinks you're a hero. Don't you see how she looks at you? She adores you."

"Not the way she adores Finn. It's different. I do the boring stuff. I get her to school, feed her, help her with homework, worry about her. I'm no Finn, that's for sure. He's never given a crap about real life. He cares about fun and horsing around. When my mother was away—that's what we call it, *away*—Finn entertained Celeste, got her laughing, made her wild and free like him. I took care of what needed to be done, and he got all the credit. That's how it's always been." *Finn always got the glory*, Matt thought. He was showy and theatrical and wonderful. Matt was good at organization and logistics, neither of which fostered admiration from a little girl. Or maybe anyone.

"You don't sound as though you like Finn all that much."

"On the contrary. He's incredible. He's vivacious and relaxed and unrestrained. Finn gets to do everything I don't, and I envy him." Even after death, Finn's online persona was certainly having a much better time than Matt was.

"So Celeste used to be more like Finn?" Julie asked.

"She did," Matt said softly. It hurt, remembering Celeste when she was spirited and nearly irrepressible in wonderful ways. Matt wasn't able to save that part of her.

"I think she's doing better, don't you? A little bit? She pitched a fit because I couldn't find the second season of *Glee* the other day. I think that's a good sign."

"What is *Glee*?" Matt didn't understand half of Julie's references.

"Don't worry about it. It's a good thing. And she's asking for trendy clothes for Christmas and wants me to take her shopping too."

"So she's becoming devoid of individuality? Exactly what I hoped for."

"Shut up. These are *good* things. Flat Finn is getting another round of hinges in a few weeks. Celeste gave me the go-ahead. Matty, don't you see how much she needs to fit in and needs friends? Can you imagine how desperately lonely she must be?"

"I can." Matt sighed. Julie could give Celeste what he couldn't. He knew nothing about this kind of stuff. "You're probably better for her than I am."

"But you do really important stuff. She needs someone like you to take care of her. Your mother is...having a hard time too, I think."

Matt nodded. Julie was starting to understand too much about this household. Maybe that was a good thing. Maybe it would bring them all closer to the truth. And maybe it would destroy them all. "I know. She is having a horrible time. Both my parents are. Why do you think she and my father are out of the house so much? They can't stand to be here." Damn it. He could feel his eyes welling up and hoped that Julie couldn't see. The way she could get to him like no one else could was both hated and much needed. Matt ran his hands through his hair. "Julie, I'm tired. I don't want to be Celeste's parent. I can't."

There. He had done it. Confessed one of the most painful truths of the aftermath. He was ashamed at how much he resented the role he had been forced to take on.

Neither of them said anything for a few minutes.

Although he couldn't take much more of this conversation, he did sense something: Julie had just healed a little piece of his pain. The way she could gently access parts of him that he'd pushed away for so long stunned him.

"Gee, this lying under the tree routine is really turning out to be fun, isn't it? Aren't you glad you're here?" As she always did, Julie knew when to pull back. It was exactly what she'd been doing with Celeste: pushing just far enough to elicit change without going too far. She was good at so much that Matt was not.

Another deep breath and another long exhale. "It has exceeded my expectations."

"Okay, let's talk about girls again."

"You're interested in girls? I had no idea. I thought you were dating that Seth character."

"You're a riot, Matt. Really. And for your information, Seth and I broke up."

"I didn't know." Julie hadn't mentioned this. Even to Finn.

"I've moved on. Sort of. I don't know what's going on. I have a crush."

Matt rolled his eyes. The stupidity around this freakish love triangle had just hit its peak. "Let me guess. My brother?"

"How did you know?" Julie seemed surprised.

This was both good and bad news. And quite confusing. "Let's see? Could it be the way you go on and on about how fabulously interesting and entertaining he is? How you check your phone for mail every three minutes? Surreptitious, you're not."

"Well, fine. So what? Anyway, we're not talking about me. We're talking about your floundering love life. Call Dana."

"I don't have time for a relationship."

"That's ridiculous. There's always time if you want it. Don't you need a little romance in your life, Matty?" Julie nudged his shoulder with her hand.

Yes, he did need a little romance in his life, but going out with her friend was not exactly what he had in mind. Matt would have to put this off as long as possible, but he could tell that she was not going to let it go. For right now, he was happy to have this perfect night with Julie.

They stayed under the tree for a bit more, talking and joking, and then, because she was leaving for California and wouldn't be here for Christmas, they exchanged gifts. The geeky T-shirts that she gave him were perfect, and she clearly loved the Dunkin' Donuts gift card that he gave her. When she flung her arms around him, laughing and hugging him tightly, Matt smiled.

For a few brief moments, Matt got to hold Julie in his arms. And that gift? That would stay with him forever.

New Year's Eve

Flat-Out Love, Chapter 22, MPOV

Matt Watkins I think I'm supposed to consult a doctor now; my ego has been swollen for WAY more than four hours.

Finn is God I wear a different deodorant scent in each armpit so I can always tell which way I'm turning if I get blindfolded and kidnapped by pirates.

Julie Seagle To be fair, if you really also meant "No pants, no service," the sign should say that.

Matt was half asleep at eleven-thirty on New Year's Eve. If he could just shut off his thoughts he could zonk out and wake up to a fresh year, a year in which things might get straightened out. Unlikely, but still. At the very least, he wanted to sleep and disappear.

Matt wasn't one for holidays, and this New Year's was particularly lonely. His parents were away, but it wasn't their absence that made the house feel so empty, because in some ways it was actually easier when they were gone.

The source of his loneliness was annoyingly clear to him. He missed Julie. She'd been in California for a week now, and he missed everything about her. The e-mailing and chatting back and forth tonight as Finn while she was at dinner waiting for her father had been fun, and he was glad that she liked the necklace, but it didn't compare to actually being around her. He was still a little surprised at himself for giving her the purple stone he'd found years ago, but it felt right for her to have it, although he wasn't sure exactly why. It represented who he used to be before he got so shut down, maybe? He wanted her to have a piece of that, even if she didn't know it was from him? Overthinking why he gave it to her wasn't going to do him any good, but he was relieved that it wasn't a disaster.

What *was* disastrous was that Matt had set things up so that someone else was wooing her and getting all the credit. Matt was an unbelievable jerk, he knew that. This wasn't intentional, he would never have wanted this, but he had gone down a rabbit hole and was now having the most messed-up tea party of all. Alice had nothing on him.

Matt took a deep breath and tried to quell the rising panic. He pulled a pillow over his head and yanked the covers up high, wanting to block out all light and sound. Trying to sort out what he felt for Julie was nearly impossible, but above everything else was the simple fact that she was his best friend. His only friend, really.

Yes, Matt had school-based friendships—acquaintanceships, really—but he never went out with friends the way his peers did. He couldn't. He worried enough as it was when he had to stay late at school, and the idea of being gone for purely social reasons seemed wrong. Besides, he preferred limiting his friendships because bringing people into his life would invariably mean twisting truths, or hiding secrets, or protecting someone. What he'd gotten himself involved in with Julie was perhaps an extreme example of stepping outside those boundaries, but it was solid proof that it was best to keep people at arm's length.

With Julie, they were all breaking the rules.

And now she was his best friend. A truth that felt awful because she obviously didn't feel the same way. She liked him well enough, he knew that, but she had friends and a life outside of this house. Matt had not invaded her world and her heart the way she had his.

His cell phone rang, jarring him out of his semiconscious depressed thinking. He pulled the pillow off his head and fumbled for his phone. He answered quickly without checking the Caller ID. Phone calls that came in at midnight had to be bad. Could something have happened to his parents?

"Hello?" General sleep deprivation combined with fear to make his voice soft and scratchy.

"What are you wearing?"

Matt relaxed. Whoever this crank caller was certainly wasn't reporting any kind of crisis. "Um... Who is this?" he said sleepily as he dropped his head back onto the pillow.

"Matty, it's me!"

He was awake now. "Julie?"

"Yes, Matty! Have you forgotten me already? What are you doing home? You should be out revelrying!" She was loud, her words running together but full of energy.

He laughed softly. She was such a nut. "I was sleeping. And *revelrying*? I'm not familiar with that term."

"Yes. It's a term because I say so. I'm creative like that. Oh my God, I'm The Terminator! Get it? Don't you miss me and my delightful banter?"

"I do miss you," he said, yawning. It was clear that he had become the victim of drunk dialing, and getting her off the phone quickly would probably be smart, although he liked hearing he was missed. "Sure."

"That's not convincing. You're hurting my feelings."

"Everybody misses you. Especially Celeste. Thanks for all the e-mails you've been sending her." Focusing on how much Celeste missed Julie was the only good move he could make here without getting into uncomfortable territory. And his sister really *was* missing Julie, so it wasn't a lie.

"Aw, my buddy Celeste." Julie made some light grunting sounds. "There. I did it!"

"You did what?"

"I got myself undressed!" So much for not getting into uncomfortable territory.

"I think you got yourself drunk, that's what I think."

"So what? So what if I'm drunk? I'm still funny."

"You are funny," he agreed. "How is California? How's your father?"

"My father is fan-frickin-tastic. He's clearly aiming for Father of the Year with the way he's spoiling me. It's a really good trip."

Even beyond the obvious and uncharacteristic alcohol consumption, Julie did not sound like herself. This level of enthusiasm was clearly forced and insincere. Matt was a bit worried about her now. "Er... Are you okay?"

"I'm perfect. Are *you* okay?"

"Yes," he said. "Are you going to make it until midnight?" Based on her faulty speech alone, passing out might be the best idea.

"Of course I'll make it to midnight," she said defensively. "I'm gonna watch fireworks shoot out over the ocean." Matt highly doubted she had the coordination skills left to get dressed again, much less figure out how to walk to find these fireworks. "Wanna come watch with me?"

He smiled to himself. He would love to. More than anything. "Sure. I'll be there in a minute. Don't start without me."

"I can always count on you, can't I, Matty? You're the best, and you're very helpful. I love you."

"Now I know you're drunk." Under other circumstances, her words might not cut so deeply, but a drunk, meaningless delivery told him how far they were from being where he wanted. She had no idea what she was saying now.

"Calm down, silly boy. Not like *I love you*-love you. I just love you. You're so smart. Oh, you love me too, and you know it."

Matt couldn't respond to this. Besides, making sure that she was safe was the only important thing. She clearly had no experience with drinking, and it was more than likely that she was going to be in terrible shape tomorrow, particularly with no one to take care of her. Where was her father? Why was she so wasted before nine o'clock California time? "Have you had any water to drink?"

"See what I mean? *That* is the smartest idea ever!" He listened to some plodding footsteps and then the sound of a faucet running. He had to laugh. Based on the sound of her walk, she must be staggering like mad. She could career to the side, ricochet off a wall, and get a concussion. Or she could just look ridiculous. It would be one or the other. "Okay, here I go. Are you ready?"

"Go for it."

"Now, hold on. Don't go anywhere."

Matt rolled his eyes. Julie had quite obviously stuck her entire face under the tap since he could hear every gulp and gasp and splash as she hydrated herself. If any of the water was making it to her mouth, he'd be shocked.

"Ta-da!" she announced.

"You also could have used a glass."

"You didn't say to, and you're the one in charge. Now I have to pee. Don't listen, because that would be gross."

Matt clapped a hand to his forehead. This was hardly the intimacy he'd been hoping for with Julie. "Believe me, I will not listen."

"You talk, and I'll pee. Talk loud to cover up the pee sound. Tell me something interesting. You always have interesting things to babble about."

"I do not babble." But Matt thanked her for the messenger bag and hinges that she'd given Celeste for Christmas. He had to give her credit because not only was Flat Finn close to being foldable enough to be totally concealed in that messenger bag, but the real gift was the time he spent with Celeste putting on the new hinges. If he knew Julie the way he thought he did, this had been her intention.

He dwelt on this as she started going on and on about something to do with how smart he was and how funny the shirts were that she'd given him for Christmas.

"I will admit that I sorta like all of your shirts," Julie said.

"Obviously when you get drunk, you lie. And talk a lot."

"I am not lying. They are actually a tiny bit adorable."

"I knew you would come around."

"I'm done peeing now."

"Thank you for letting me know."

He heard her stumble around again. "I look crazy. I think I should go to bed now."

"Probably a good idea. Happy New Year." Matt started to pull the phone from his ear.

"Wait, don't hang up yet! Tuck me in."

What in the world was drunk Julie talking about now? "Tuck you in?"

"Yes. Tuck me in. Come to bed with me. Oh, wait, that's not right, is it? Can you imagine?"

"Imagine what?"

"If we went to bed together. That would be bananas, huh?"

Matt sighed. Julie must be entirely out of her mind if she was mentioning the two of them in bed together. Not that he disliked that line of thinking, but.... Well, anyway, Julie was clearly a mess right now. "This conversation has officially taken an alarming turn."

"You're just figuring that out now?" She was silent for a few moments. "Matty?"

"Yes, Julie?"

"I have to tell you something."

"Go ahead."

"I like math."

"I think that is wonderful." Drunken thinking or not, he was happy to hear this. Matt had helped Julie with enough of her homework to know that, despite her near constant grumblings, she really had an aptitude for math.

"And there's something else."

"Shoot." Maybe she had a secret physics fetish too? One could always hope.

Julie lowered her voice to a whisper. "I'm a virgin."

"Oh my God, Julie, I'm hanging up now." Why in the world was she telling him this? This felt really inappropriate. Except... Matt couldn't deny a stupid level of relief. He assumed that she'd been with Seth, if not somebody before that, and he had hated thinking about what she'd been doing every time that she'd gone out with Seth for the night. Learning that they'd broken up had given him an embarrassingly good feeling. It's not as though he, or "Finn" for that matter, had any right to expect her not to have a love life. He just didn't like it.

"I'm serious," she continued, undeterred. "This is important. I'm a freshman in college. How can I still be a virgin, huh? Nobody else is a virgin. Nobody else in the whole world. What about you? You can't be. I mean, you had that girlfriend and everything. And you're old."

"Thank you."

"Well, not old. But older than I am. So you definitely can't be a virgin, right? Tell me. You've had sex, right?"

"I don't think we should be talking about this."

"Come on! Don't be such a baby. It's a perfectly normal question."

Matt rolled onto his back and tucked his hand under his head. She probably wouldn't even remember this conversation, so what the hell. "Fine. Yes, I've had sex."

"I knew it!" she yelled with a level of satisfaction that he found somehow flattering. "Have you had a lot of sex?"

Matt laughed. "I suppose it depends how you define *a lot.*"

"That means you have! Man, at the rate I'm going, I'm never going to have sex."

"Are you in a big rush?" The thought of Julie being careless with herself and her body didn't sit well. Even though she hadn't slept with Seth, what if she ran off and slept with someone from school just to get it over with? That wouldn't be right. It shouldn't be something to just hurry up and cross off a list. He knew the pressure, especially in college, not to be a virgin, but Julie should have better than some meaningless one-night stand with a random guy. Julie deserved respect, and love, and care. Tenderness. She should be with someone who would make her first time amazing. Someone who would make her feel absolutely perfect emotionally and physically. Who would take his time with her body, finding out what she liked ....

Of course, Matt was sort of going off the rails here. Getting protective over Julie wasn't his place. And she may be drunk right now, but Julie wouldn't make a wrong decision when she did decide to have sex. Behind the haze of alcohol was an incredibly smart person who would find a guy who loved her with everything he had. A non-geeky guy who hadn't developed a split personality.

"Why wouldn't I be? Everyone says sex is great. It is, isn't it?"

"I don't know that I qualify as an expert, but, yes, it can be great. If you're with the right person." Matt was silent for a moment. There were a few times when he was with Ellen that had felt right—really right—but now he wondered. What he thought had been so good maybe wasn't what it could be. Or should be. Maybe it had just been that Ellen had been his first, and the two of them had certainly taken every opportunity to rip each other's clothes off, but... that didn't necessarily make sex magical. It just meant that they'd been horny teenagers. He had cared about her a lot, but those feelings didn't compare to what he was feeling these days. Or what he was fighting not to feel.

"So you and Seth never...?" Matt couldn't help it. He had to confirm this.

"Ha! I knew you'd want to talk about this stuff! No, we never did. I didn't want to. Seth was cute and nice and perfect and all that, but I didn't want to. He just wasn't *the* guy, you know? I want *the* guy. The everything guy. Not the dumb Prince Charming, nauseatingly-perfect-everything guy. That's pathetic. I want the flaws-and-all, everything guy."

Matt was indeed not a Prince Charming kind of a guy, but he was pretty sure that "flaws-and-all" did not include pretending to be your dead brother and seducing a girl via e-mails and chats. Still, one never knew.... "You'll find him. Not when you're drunk and slurring, but you'll find him." Julie deserved this guy who she was drunkenly dreaming about. He sounded a lot better than Matt.

"Hey, they're counting down to midnight. In stupid New York where all the stupid cool people are. Let's count together."

She must have Times Square on her television. Matt wasn't sure what she had against all of New York, but if this countdown meant that she would get to sleep and start the recovery process, he was all for it. She was going to feel wretched in the morning. "Tell me when."

"Seven, six..." she said, and Matt started to count with her. "Five, four, three, two, one!"

He heard cheering and music in the background. "Happy New Year, Julie."

"Happy New Year, Matty." It was quiet. "Matty, I have another question for you."

"Uh-oh."

"Are you a skilled lover?" The seriousness of her tone was beyond words.

"And that concludes our evening chat."

"I bet I could be a skilled lover. I'm very energetic. And a quick learner."

He really couldn't take this. The last thing he needed was Julie's oversharing about her sexual potential contributing to fantasies that he was already routinely pushing away. "You definitely need to go to sleep."

"Oh, fine. I can't stay on the phone anymore. I have to get to sleep."

"I think that's a good plan. I'm glad you thought of it."

"I like talking to you," Julie mumbled.

He smiled again. That simple phrase meant the world to him, whether she meant it or not. This entire conversation was likely to fall into the wasteland of forgotten drunk memories. Which was probably a good thing. "I like talking to you too. Most of the time. I'll see you when you get back."

"G'night, Matty."

He hung up the phone and set it on the floor next to his bed. That was either the best or the worst conversation he'd ever had with a girl. It was an eerie parallel to the general Julie situation: she would either be the best or the worst girl to come into his life. He would find out. He didn't know when, but he would find out.

The Polar Plunge

Flat-Out Love, Chapter 23, MPOV

Matt Watkins took over a year to learn how to walk after he first left the hospital. But he never lost faith in himself, even at that early age.

Finn is God You mock me for my apathetic nature, but meh.

Julie Seagle I bet the very first piñata was surprised. "Oh, hey a party! Cool! What's the occa— HEY, WHAT THE HELL, KID?"

Matt sat up in bed, wide awake and panicked. He touched a hand to his chest. He was sweating. It was still dark out, but he knew he wouldn't go back to sleep. Something felt wrong. He threw on sweatpants, tucked his phone into the pocket, and tiptoed into the hall. The house was quiet, and Celeste's door was still shut, but he quietly opened it and checked on his sister. She was still asleep. But something had woken him. He crossed the hall to Julie's room and checked in there. Matt flipped on the light. The room was empty.

Obviously it was empty. She was in California. And probably still drunk. He hoped she would sleep most of the day so that she wouldn't have to be awake for a good portion of the nausea and headache that were bound to hit this morning. He sat down on her bed. Being in her room was comforting. And also sad. He flopped back on the bed and looked up at the ceiling.

He lay there unmoving until light started to filter in through the windows. He was waiting. Waiting for what, he didn't know, but there was most definitely a charge in the air that had him on high alert.

His phone sounded and he pulled it from his pocket. It was a message from Julie to Finn, simply quoting an In Like Lions song that had come up in one of their chats. Yup, she was still drunk. Probably stumbling around in search of water and aspirin before she crashed back asleep.

Matt got up and went downstairs. The kitchen floor was freezing and he regretted not having thrown on socks. A relentless chill swallowed the entire house today. It was wretched out: gray skies, frigid temperatures, and the threat of snow. So much for a spectacular start to the new year. He put the tea kettle on the stove and filled the French press with espresso grounds. The house was too quiet, even when the water boiled and the room filled with the kettle's sharp whistle.

Matt stared at the steam. Lyrics swirled in his head.

I was broken... I am broken... Ride the wave be gone... Save me, come save me....

Oh, hell. Julie's e-mail wasn't drunken nonsense.

He lifted the kettle from the burner and slammed it down before turning off the heat. "Damn it, Julie! Damn it!"

Matt was upstairs and in Celeste's room in a heartbeat. "Celeste, we have to go. Come on! Get dressed!"

A mass of curls stuck out from underneath the sheets. "Matty? I would prefer not to go anywhere right now as I am sleeping, and I suspect it is cold and despicable outside. I have a fondness for meteorology, and based on what I heard last night—"

"Get! Up!" Matt pulled down the sheets and tugged at Celeste's flannel pajama top.

"Where is it that we must go at this early hour? What is of such an urgent nature?"

"It's Julie. She's doing something stupid and dangerous, and we have to get her. Let's go!"

Celeste's eyes opened wide. "Oh! We are off on an exciting rescue mission, is that correct?"

"Yes." Matt reached into a laundry basket of clean clothes and tossed jeans and a heavy sweater at Celeste. "Here. Just put these on over what you're wearing. We have to go now."

"Matthew?" Celeste sat up and started pulling the jeans over her long underwear.

"What?" he asked, exasperated at how slow she was.

"Do you think that perhaps you too should put on some clothes?"

Matt looked down. She had a point. He might need to wear something besides only sweatpants. "Yeah, okay. Fine. Just hurry."

Matt raced to his room, snatched some clothes from his dresser, and put on a T-shirt as he stumbled down the stairs, falling hard onto the landing. He slid his feet into socks and shoes, swearing too loudly. "Move it, Celeste!" he yelled. "And grab some warm clothes for Julie!"

Celeste followed him to the foyer, where he grabbed the car keys and Julie's boots. "This is a remarkably exciting way to start the day, isn't it?" she asked happily.

Matt yanked a wool hat over her head. "No. No, it is not."

They rushed through the frozen snow to the car. Matt cursed the old Volvo that was taking forever to heat up enough to drive. He could feel Celeste's eyes boring into him expectantly.

"What is it?" he snapped.

"Are we going to the airport and flying to California? I do not want to go on an airplane. Not at all. But I will if we are to partake in a heroic cross-country mission."

"No, we're not flying anywhere." Matt turned on the wipers and cranked up the air, willing the windows to defrost enough so that he could see. "Julie is in Boston. I don't think she ever left."

"Why is she not with her father? Why did she not tell us? Where has she been staying?"

"I don't know," he whispered. "Something must have happened."

"And what is this apparently stupid and dangerous activity in which she is engaging?" Celeste folded the clothes she had for Julie into a neat pile on her lap.

"She is doing the goddamn Polar Plunge." He was so mad that he could hardly speak the words aloud.

"Is this a bear-related activity? That does indeed sound quite dangerous."

"What? No, it's not a bear-related activity." He wiped the window with his glove and then backed the car out of the driveway. "She's jumping into the Atlantic Ocean with a bunch of other insane people. It's a New Year's Day event. The water is freezing. "

"How do you know that she is doing this?"

"I just... do."

"Because you know her?" Celeste asked softly.

Matt took a moment before he responded. "Yes. Because I know her." And he knew that Julie wanted to do this Plunge because Finn had done it. Really, Matt and Finn had done it together. A matter of weeks before Finn died.

"I do not think that sounds like an enjoyable activity in the least, but I also feel strongly that Julie must have a solid reason for participating in this cold-water plunging festival."

"It's not a festival! And there is no good reason!" Matt looked at the clock. They might make it in time to stop her. Maybe. The ocean water could shut down her body. The current could pull her under. He knew the way the icy water felt as though it were burning your skin, and how the shock of the cold could energize you. It could also debilitate you. Matt and Finn had known how to handle the rush, plus they kept an eye on each other. Julie wouldn't know what to do with the shock, and there was no one there to watch over her. Matt didn't care that paramedics were present because in the wild crowd it would be easy to miss one girl vanishing into the dark ocean. "God, Julie, what the hell are you doing?" he yelled out.

Celeste calmly retied her scarf. "It is my opinion that you are having an unreasonably strong reaction to how Julie has chosen to celebrate this holiday."

"I'll react however I want to when someone does something so alarmingly outrageous."

"Do you mean when a woman who you desire to engage with above a friendship level does something so alarmingly—"

"Celeste! Stop it," Matt growled. He was not in the mood to wrangle Celeste's dramatizations right now. He took a plastic baggie from his coat pocket and held it out. "Here, I have a muffin that I took to school the other day. You should eat something."

"I do not want a muffin."

"Yes, you do." He tapped his fingers on the steering wheel.

"No, I do not want a muffin."

Matt shook the bag wildly. "Just eat the muffin, okay?" he demanded. "You're supposed to have breakfast!"

Celeste took the bag from his hand. "Goodness. If eating the muffin will help alleviate this display of emotionality, I will be happy to accommodate you and eat the muffin." She paused. "I would be happier if you had not sat on it and if it were not undeniably compressed into a near pancake."

"JUST EAT THE FREAKIN' MUFFIN!" Matt flew through an intersection.

"It is my suspicion that by *freakin'* you really mean *fu*—"

"How about we stop talking, okay?"

"Yes. Let's. I will eat my subpar, unusually shaped muffin disc now." She patted his shoulder. "And we will find Julie, and she will be perfectly fine."

Matt took a deep breath. "I know."

They drove silently to the beach in South Boston.

Matt took the first parking space he could find and slammed the car to a stop. "I'm sorry that I yelled at you, Celeste," he said.

"I know. I do not mind much as the source of your outburst that elicited such an elevated reaction is near and dear to us both." She opened her door and stepped out.

Matt shut off the ignition. He looked around the car, cursing himself for not having thought to bring towels, but he was relieved to see a blanket in the back. He grabbed it and opened his door, darting out to run through the parking lot and toward the beach. The sand slowed his pace, but he pushed ahead as fast as he could with Celeste trailing after him.

"Look at all the swimmers, Matty! This is delightful!"

The crowd on the beach was infuriating, and he weaved angrily around cheering people who clearly were not the least bit concerned about their loved ones who were in the Atlantic Ocean in January. He and Celeste finally got in front of the other onlookers, and he scanned the water, now full of barely dressed swimmers splashing around. "Where is she? Where is she? Do you see her?"

"There! I believe that is her." Celeste pointed a bit to their right. "She is wearing a bikini. A very small one."

It was Julie. He would know her anywhere. She ran through deep blue waves and then suddenly threw her whole body under water. Matt dropped the blanket and flew forward to the edge of the water. "Julie!" he called. He kept his eyes on her, but knelt down and started to untie his boots. He was going in after her.

"No, Matty. Let her do this."

"Celeste, she's going to drown."

"No, she is *not* going to drown. She wants this experience. Give it to her."

Julie burst through to the surface before diving under for a second time. She was crazy. Matt stood up and cupped his hands by his mouth and yelled out her name again.

Sleet was falling, and the sky was darkening as deep gray clouds took over the sky. He watched as she stood in waist-level water and slowly began to drop. The cold had gotten to her, he knew. She was going under now, and not by her own will.

When you are numb, you lose control, you lose reason, you lose care.

"Julie!" Matt screamed as loudly as he could. He began to unzip his coat.

Celeste grabbed his arm. "No, Matthew. It is all right. There is someone there."

Matt shook with relief as an older, muscular man with a frizzy white ponytail lifted Julie into his arms just before she disappeared under the dark water. Matt and Celeste waved their arms at the man and he carried Julie their way. Celeste handed Matt the blanket, and he held it open. The older man neared them with a smile. Julie was so frozen that she didn't even look their way. "This girl belong to you?"

Matt nodded wordlessly, and the man set Julie's feet gently on the sand in front of them before he disappeared into the crowd. Relief rushed through Matt as he wrapped the blanket around Julie. She was shaking in his arms, her body fighting frantically to warm up.

He held her tightly, rubbing her arms. "Oh my God, Julie! What were you doing?"

"Matt? Did you see me?" She buried her head against him.

"Yeah. I saw you." He couldn't conceal his anger.

"Did you see Santa Claus, too?" She was hoarse from the cold.

"That wasn't Santa Claus. That was one of the L Street Brownies who rescued you from certain death. It was considerate of him, after you crashed their event." Matt tightened the blanket around her and started furiously rubbing her back. "We have to get you warmed up. Dummy. Hey, can you get her sweatpants and socks and boots on? Hurry."

Celeste helped Julie move her legs into her clothes. "I saw you, too, and I thought you were brilliant! Really stupendous!"

"Celeste?" Julie tried to turn her head, but Matt kept his arms around her, keeping the blanket over her wet hair and protecting her from the wind. He could hear her teeth chattering through the blanket, for God's sake, and he was livid with her for doing this to herself.

"I'm here!" Celeste said excitedly. "I'm attending to your blue feet!"

"Why are you here? How?" Julie asked.

Matt lowered the blanket for a moment so that he could pull the shirt and sweatshirt they'd brought over her head. What was she thinking, wearing this tiny bikini out in public? She was lucky that she hadn't been mauled by horny swimmers. Even nearly blue, she was gorgeous. Anyone would think so. Julie met his eyes finally, and he frowned as he wrapped the blanket back around her.

"Finn figured it out. He sent me to get you," he whispered into her ear. "What the hell were you thinking? We could see you standing out there in the ocean, not moving. You're lucky you're not dead. Goddamn it, Julie. Why would you do that? Why are you here and not in California with your father?" He was angry and he couldn't hide it.

Julie dropped her head forward and leaned into him. "Because he's a jerk, and I'm a liar." Her voice caught and she started sobbing.

Matt didn't say anything, but he kept rubbing her back. Celeste moved behind Julie, pressing her between them. Matt didn't know what to say, so he let Julie's tears fall while he and Celeste held her.

"Please don't cry, Julie. You were simply wonderful out there," Celeste said.

"She was not wonderful, Celeste. She was a dope." Matt managed to soften his tone. "But we're glad you're okay. You are okay, aren't you? I mean... physically?" Clearly she was a mental basket case right now.

Julie nodded and then turned her head, still resting it against Matt's chest. He was relieved beyond words that she was safe.

"Matt?"

"Yeah?"

"Did we talk on the phone last night?"

He paused. Oh, no. "We did."

"Did I ask you...?" Julie seemed to fumble for words. "Did I ask you if you were a *skilled lover*?"

Matt cleared his throat and paused again. He'd been hoping that conversation was lost forever. "You did."

Celeste burst out laughing.

Julie tucked her head down lower. "Sorry."

"Let's get you into the car. It should still be warm."

"Celeste, can you grab my bag?" Julie pointed from under the blanket to the benches on the other side of the beach.

"Absolutely. Hey, Julie?"

"Yeah, kiddo?"

"I'm glad that you're here." Celeste beamed. "Home."

"Me too."

"Meet us at the car, okay?" Matt stepped away from Julie and turned her in the direction of the street. *Home.* Celeste was right. Julie's home was with them.

"So, Matt," she started and looked up at him smiling. God, he'd missed that smile. "Last night? What was your answer?"

"I'm not going to tell you. Now maybe you won't drink so much again."

Julie sighed. "Believe me. Lesson learned."

Matt got her into the front seat and cranked up the heat. Celeste bounded into the car with Julie's bag, and they started the drive home. The frozen girl in the seat next to him periodically shuddered and held her hands in front of the car vents that didn't seem to be producing enough heat for even a mildly chilly day.

Matt frowned and fiddled with the controls, finally hitting the dashboard. He wanted hot air blasting onto Julie immediately. "Come on! Come on, you piece of crap!" He slammed his hand down again.

"It's all right. Calm down. I'm warming up," Julie insisted.

"No, you're not fine." Matt was angry again. "That was a stupid thing to do. It was reckless. Seriously, what would possess you?"

Julie leaned back. "I don't care. I'm glad I did it."

"It's called a *plunge*. It's not a *stand-in-the-dangerously-cold-water-and-stare-fixedly-at-nothing* event. A plunge means exactly that. You plunge in and get the hell out. Not that you should have even been doing that."

"Yes, sir."

"I'm not fooling around, Julie. That was stupid. Stupid." Matt hit the gas, desperate to get Julie back to the house where he could take care of her properly. He would build a fire, and make her soup, and force her to drink lots of fluids. Hot tea, maybe? He was sure there was a wool blanket in the linen closet upstairs....

"Slow down, Matt!" Julie said hoarsely. "You're going to get a ticket."

"I'll drive as fast as I want. The quicker we get you home, the quicker you can warm up."

"Why don't you just take me back to Dana's? Turn left up here."

"Is that where you've been staying?" He was really pissed off now. If her father blew her off, why would she stay at Dana's and not with them? Had she even left Boston at all? And if she thought for two seconds that he would drop her off at an empty apartment, then she had surely frozen most of her brain cells in the Atlantic. Her lack of responsibility was appalling. "No. I am not taking you back to Dana's. Who knows what other trouble you'll get yourself into?"

"Matt! I can stay wherever I want to. I'm an adult."

"You're not acting like it."

"Why do you care where I stay?"

"Ah, a lovers' quarrel," Celeste said dreamily from the back seat.

"Shut up!" Matt and Julie yelled together.

No one spoke for the rest of the ride home.

Later, when Julie had taken a long, hot shower, and Celeste was in her room, Matt was starting to relax. He really snapped at Julie on the car ride home, but now that she was safe at home, curled up in front of a blazing fire on the living room floor with her head on a pillow, he felt better.

What a morning. He still couldn't believe that he and Celeste left the house without Flat Finn. It was quite an accomplishment, intentional or not. For Celeste, of course, but maybe for him too. He felt guilty for forgetting his sister's flat obsession, but it was also a good thing. His neurosis about that ridiculous cardboard thing was probably as pathological as hers. Today he and Celeste were reminded that there was a world outside of Flat Finn in which other things—other people—took precedence. Matt poked at the fire, sending flames shooting up. Good. He wanted the hottest fire possible.

He listened while Julie explained about her father canceling their trip and how she was too embarrassed to tell him. As much as Matt wanted to rip off her father's head for what he'd done to his daughter, he contained his anger for her sake. Julie nudged him about Roger and Erin leaving him and Celeste alone, but this time he didn't mind talking about his family or his feelings. Well, not as much as he usually minded. Maybe the heat from the fire was getting to him.

"I'm sorry your parents left you here alone. That's not very nice."

Matt jabbed the fire with an iron poker. "No, it's not very nice, is it? And I'm sorry your dad left *you* alone. That's also not very nice."

"Thanks." Julie closed her eyes. Between last night's alcohol and this morning's chaos, she must be wiped out.

"Tired, huh? Why don't you sleep for a while?"

Matt got up and pulled the curtains shut in the living room, and then he covered her with the wool blanket. Julie yawned and turned onto her side so that she was facing the fireplace. "Did you call Dana?"

"Not yet. I will." He didn't want to, but Julie would be relentless about this.

"Thanks for getting me, Matty. I'm sorry," she mumbled.

"Of course. It's not a problem." He sat down next to her, watching her breathing begin to slow as her drowsiness took over and her eyes closed.

Even now, in front of the fire, she shivered in her sleep. Without thinking, Matt lay on his side next to her and propped himself up on one arm. For a few minutes, he just took her in. Then he scooted forward slightly, wanting to warm her with his body, wanting to be as close to her as possible, and wanting to protect her even though the danger had passed. She rolled back against him, touching her back to his chest. Slowly and gently, he ran the back of his hand over her cheek. The color had returned. She was all right.

What had today been about for her? Was she trying to prove something to Finn? To herself? That she could... what? Do something brave?

Independent? Matt shook his head. Julie didn't have to do a Polar Plunge for him to know she was brave and independent. He leaned his head in, barely touching his forehead to her cheek as he whispered the lyrics she sent to Finn this morning.

Said I'm fallin', too cold in my town... Said I'm breathin', but I don't know how.

Matt closed his eyes as an understanding washed over him. He was in love.

It didn't matter, though.

She would never see it, and she would never want him.

It had taken just four short months, and now he was painfully in love.

You got the sweetest eyes to ever look my way. Come save me... Come save me.

Matt lifted his head and looked at Julie while she slept. He pulled away, laying on his side again and resting his head in his hand. If anything had happened to her today.... Maybe he was overreacting, as Celeste had accused him. But seeing Julie out there in the strong ocean, challenging herself to battle the paralyzing cold and the unpredictable waves, had most certainly scared him. More than that, however, he was impressed with her strength. Although her father hurt her—probably more deeply than she explained to Matt—she fought to reclaim control by doing something that was likely scary for her. Her method may have been a bit extreme, and Matt was still angry and shaken up, but he still respected her for it.

For the first time he saw that she was more alone than he thought. Not the way that he was, but still....

He could see it because he knew that lonely people hide secrets more than others.

Celeste had Flat Finn to watch over her, and now Julie had Matt. At least for now. For however long she slept.

Follow the wheel that makes your heart move, ride the wave be gone. Ride the wave be gone, ride the wave be gone, ride the wave be gone....

The Sleepover

Flat-Out Love, Chapters 25/ 26, MPOV

Matt Watkins Of course I'd be happy to give you my opinion because it increases the odds of me being able to say, "I told you so" in the future.

Finn is God What's that mental disorder where you believe that you're the only real person in the world? I'm asking for an imaginary friend.

Julie Seagle says you may call it "plagiarizing from the classics," but I call it "collaborating with the dead." (Clearly I'm not into this mid-term project.)

Matt finally took Julie's friend Dana out on a date. It was the only way to get Julie to stop nagging him, and the more she nagged, the more he saw how useless it was to hold out hope that she might entertain the possibility of anything between the two of them. While he had a nice enough time on the date, it wasn't until the end of the evening that he saw what a total jackass he really was.

There was nothing wrong with Dana. She was just as great as Julie promised. Pretty, too. It was easy to keep a conversation going with her over dinner, and she made him laugh a few times. He drove her back to her apartment, parked under a streetlamp, and then he kissed her. Slowly. It wasn't impulsive, but rather his attempt to redirect the constant ache that plagued him. He had to move on. So he kept his eyes closed while he teased her lips with his, and while he touched his tongue to hers. He missed kissing someone. He missed touch and being touched. For twenty minutes he made out with Dana, kissing her, building it slowly, until they were both heated and gasping. He put one hand on the back of her neck and let his fingers move into her hair while he drowned in her and tried to forget. His other hand slid to her back where he delicately lifted the hem of her loose blouse. He traced the line of the top her skirt with one finger, just barely touching her skin and making her pull away to gasp for air. Dana put her hands on his chest, moving over his shirt, soon digging her fingers into him. It had been way too long since anyone had touched him like this. Matt rounded his hand over the curve of her hip, softly putting the palm of his hand against her, then inched up her waist, under her shirt... and up higher, until he was cupping her breast in his hand. She kissed him harder, and Matt responded, curling his fingers around the silk at the top of her bra and ducking his touch under the fabric. Then he was pushing the straps from her shoulders. His mouth moved from hers, and soon he was kissing her neck, working his way lower.

And that's when he murmured Julie's name.

It was awful.

Dana was very kind about it, but it was an inexcusable thing to have done, even for a twenty-year-old guy who was in the worst dry spell in the history of dry spells. And this wasn't him. He wasn't the guy who slept around, indulging in whatever one-night fling he could. Matt didn't do that, and he didn't want that.

With one hand under his chin, Dana lifted his head. "I thought so."

Matt froze.

She smiled. "You've got it bad, don't you?"

Matt didn't answer that. He didn't have to.

"It's okay, Matt. I'm not upset. You talked about her all through dinner—obsessively so, if I might point out—so I'm not exactly surprised." She paused and ruffled his hair with her hand. Damn. How could he not have been aware that every topic they'd covered had led him to mention Julie? Dana lifted an eyebrow. "She doesn't know, does she?"

Matt looked away.

"It's okay. I won't tell her, I promise. That's up to you."

He slumped back into the driver's seat and dropped his head. "I'm so sorry. I don't know what happened there. I shouldn't have—"

"Stop worrying." She put a hand on his shoulder. "I knew what was happening. I just thought we'd have some fun. It wasn't a great idea. We're both not over other people, and we were trying to forget."

"Didn't work out very well for us, did it?" Matt managed to laugh softly.

"It never does. Although there *were* some damn good moments there." Dana laughed. "Julie ought to pay more attention."

Matt looked out the windshield at the empty street. "That's not going to happen."

"Give it time. You're too far gone for this not to work out."

****

It was nearly midnight, and Matt and Julie had been talking and listening to music since he dropped off Celeste at Rachel's house for a sleepover. Only Julie could take his mind off of the fact that his sister was away from home for the night. For the first time. Rachel and her mother seemed nice enough, and Julie was positive that this would be a complete success, so Matt was trying to relax and not think about the possibilities. Flat Finn was folded up and hidden away in Celeste's bag, but what if one of the other girls found him? Or what if someone made fun of Celeste for... for any myriad of things? His sister's confidence on the drive over was helpful, though. She was ready for this step, thanks to Julie, so Matt would be ready too.

It was a nice evening. Roger and Erin were away again for the weekend, off enjoying the mid-spring weather, so Matt and Julie had the house to themselves. Hanging out with Julie was always fun, even if it was just a night of friendship.

Julie was wrapping up a phone call, and Matt was pretending not to know that she was pressing Dana for date details via a poorly disguised conversation about a nonexistent study group. That's what he got for not answering Julie's probing questions about his date, and he could only hope that Dana didn't throw him under the bus. Julie did nearly drop the phone at one point, so he could only imagine what she'd heard.

"Sorry," Julie hung up. "Important stuff about my study group."

"Sounded like it. I'm going to get something to drink." Matt stood up. "And how's Dana?"

"Oh." Julie looked away, but he saw her blush. "Ahem. She's fine. Sorry."

The house phone rang, and Matt left his room to locate the handset. Julie's interest in his date made it hard to suppress a smile. It didn't mean that she was on the verge of throwing herself at him in a jealous fit, but he didn't mind if Dana revealed one or two things to Julie, nor if those things had touched even the smallest jealous nerve.

He was in such a good mood that it didn't occur to him to worry about getting a midnight phone call. "Hello?"

It didn't matter that Rachel's mother spoke in a steady, gentle voice as she relayed that Celeste was in tears—hysterics, really—and that she needed to be picked up. The room started spinning as Matt listened to the voice on the other end of the phone explain that his sister was still on the floor of the bathroom, unable to stop crying or shaking. It also didn't matter that the other girls were asleep and didn't know. Nothing mattered except getting to Celeste. He flew downstairs and ran his hands over the small cubby shelves in the kitchen in search of the car keys. He could barely see straight.

"Matt?"

"Where the hell are my keys?" He touched his jean pockets and then scanned the countertops.

"I think they're hanging by the front door. Where are you going?"

Matt rushed past her, and she followed him into the front hallway.

He snatched the keys from the hook in the foyer and then stopped as he grabbed the door handle, turning around and facing her, furious. "I told you. God *damn* it, I told you, Julie!" He was screaming at her now.

She took a step back. "What are you talking about?"

"Rachel's mother just called from the party. Celeste is having a meltdown."

"What happened?" Julie took her sweatshirt off of the coat rack and started to follow him out. "She seemed so sure of herself."

"No!" he said pointing at her. "You are not coming with me." He would be happy never to see her again.

"Matt? Please. I can help. I can talk—"

"No! *You* did this, *I'll* fix it." If he could. If Celeste wasn't too far gone. Who knows what happened at the party that sent her spiraling. Matt slammed the door behind him. He couldn't think clearly, all he could do was react.

He drove calmly, paying careful attention to his driving. Collecting a nearly incapacitated Celeste happened in a daze. The frighteningly loud sobbing that she was able to contain at Rachel's house erupted in the car, and all he could do was keep her hand in his while he drove and tell her over and over again that everything would be okay. It wouldn't be okay, but he told her that anyway.

Somehow he was in the house, blowing past Julie, and carrying his sister to her bedroom. He tucked her under the sheets and rubbed her back. Celeste was inconsolable, unable to talk, so he just stayed with her and sat through the awful wails as his rage mounted. Listening to his sister's agony was nearly intolerable. This was Julie's fault. Her expectations were careless and thoughtless. She had asked for too much from Celeste, and this was the result.

Later, when Celeste was nearly spent of tears, she rolled to face him. "I am sorry, Matthew. I am so very sorry." Speaking was a struggle right now, he could see that. Her fragility wrecked him.

"There's nothing to be sorry for. You're home now, everything is fine." He wiped the tears on her face with his thumbs. "Take some long, deep breaths. Can you do that for me? Like this."

She studied his face and inhaled and exhaled along with him, over and over, until she could speak. She even smiled a little. "Sometimes, for instance right now, you look like him. Did you know that?"

Matt shook his head. "No, I don't. Don't say that."

"Yes. You really do. I see it in your eyes. And in the way you tip your head to the side when you are worried. But you can stop worrying now. I feel much better."

"Good. I'm glad. You should go to sleep now, don't you think?" He should ask her to tell him what happened. He knew that. But he just couldn't. He wasn't equipped for this conversation. Once again, he was helpless.

"Yes, I must sleep, but first I would like to speak to Julie."

Matt clenched his jaw. "You can talk to her tomorrow."

"I would like to speak to her now. I need to."

"If that's what you want." He leaned down and kissed her forehead. "I'll see you in the morning. I'm sorry about all of this. This was a mistake." Matt took her hand in both of his for a moment as he struggled to find the right words to tell her that he loved her, and that he would do anything to trade places with Finn so that she could have the brother she really loved back with her. There was no way to say that, so he just kept her hand in his for a minute more. "Good night, Celeste."

The hallway was dimly lit, but it was still easy to see the distress on Julie's face. Matt didn't care. She deserved to be miserable.

"Matt? Oh, God. I don't know what—"

He held up his hand. "Don't say anything to me. She wants to talk to you." Matt brushed past her coldly as she carried Flat Finn into Celeste's room. He leaned against the wall and crossed his arms while he began to come undone in his own way. Never had he been this angry with anyone. How had he trusted someone else to step into Celeste's world? Of the many mistakes he'd made, allowing Julie to push Celeste too far was the worst one of all. Matt leaned against the wall in the hallway, his expression icy and distant.

By the time Julie left Celeste's bedroom, his rage was barely contained. Matt didn't even want to look at her. He was disgusted with her and with himself. When she stepped close to him, he snapped. "Stay away from me. I can't deal with you right now."

"Matt...."

"I swear to God, don't talk to me now. Don't."

"I'm so sorry. You have no idea."

"I don't want to hear it. I don't want to hear anything from you."

"Matt, you know I love Celeste, and I would never have done anything to hurt her."

"Well, you did."

"If you would just let me explain again why—"

"You don't stop, do you? You want to get into this? Fine. Let's get into it. You thought you could just show up here and insinuate yourself into our lives? You can't. And you also can't act like I'm the bad guy. Like everything I do for her is somehow totally brainless." He moved so that he was facing her, placing his body inches from hers. "I've busted my ass to keep Celeste in a stable place, and you just ruined it. You ruined *her*. God, Julie. You're here for a few months, and you think that you know what is right for Celeste? Nobody asked you to fix anything. You can't." He ran his hands through his hair as he continued to unleash on her, not recognizing his own voice. "You can't change this. And your constant reminders that you think we're all completely crazy are not helpful. Do you get that? What is wrong with you? Don't you have your own life to attend to? Or is this how you make yourself feel better about your crappy father, huh? You excuse the way he treats you for no good reason, and you love him based on nothing more than a few lousy e-mails a year."

Matt couldn't stop. He continued his vicious attack, hardly hearing himself or her, and speaking with no filter as he let free every ounce of anger.

When he was done, when he had torn her to the ground, he walked to his bedroom. "Go to hell, Julie."

He shut the door, turned off the light, and got into bed. Despite the chill, he took off his T-shirt, one that Julie liked, and threw it across the room. It felt like an eternity went by as he lay on his back, in shock over everything that just transpired. Everything that he said. The fear that engulfed him tonight was more than any he'd felt before. Even when Finn died. It wasn't about fear then, just grief. Deep, merciless grief. The fears around Celeste had built slowly and steadily over time, but they were different from tonight's. That phone call.... Matt thought his heart might have stopped. And now it wouldn't stop pounding.

He thought for a while, sorting through the things he yelled at Julie out in the hall. Striking out about her relationship with her father was cruel and unfair. It wasn't his place, and he shouldn't have even broached the subject tonight of all nights. Who was he to comment on parent-child relationships? Then he taunted her about Finn, about playing it safe and hiding online. Matt was a hypocrite.

Celeste is not your job. We're not your job. We're not your family.

Oh God, what had he done?

He'd been blaming Julie for all of this. But he was wrong about why. It wasn't that Julie had gone too far with Celeste—or with Matt. It was that she had given them somewhere to fall from. They hadn't had that in years. There hadn't been anything else to lose until now. He was angry with her for giving him hope because now the crash hurt like hell.

I'll never be what you want. You don't like me? Then stay out of my life.

He didn't want Julie out of his life. But he didn't know if he wanted her in it. She pushed. God, she pushed so hard. It felt as though she disapproved of so much about Matt, but he could see that wasn't the full truth. She did like him, but she also saw all of his shortcomings that he was already so painfully aware of. But maybe she pushed because she saw potential in all of them to live more vibrant, functional lives? Even him? Matt blinked back tears and tucked an arm under his head.

Everything was going to explode soon. He could feel it. There wasn't much time left. Julie was right when she said that they couldn't keep avoiding the real world. This false one was going to disintegrate, and he wouldn't be able to stop it. It would happen by the end of the school year. He'd essentially set that deadline in a chat with Julie by telling her that Finn would be home for the summer. Matt needed this to be over. It all felt like too much.

His dark room was too empty, the quiet acutely painful. The clock on his nightstand clicked loudly while he lay still and waited for the worst of his agony to pass. He was good at squashing emotions, but tonight was tough.

Later, the door opened slowly. "Matt?" And then she was there, sitting on his bed. In the moonlight, he could see that she looked as wrecked as he felt. "Matty?"

His anger and his fear still hovered, but he looked at her.

"I'm sorry. Please. You have to forgive me." Julie's voice was breaking. "I'm so sorry. I'm so sorry," she kept repeating. "Matty, please. You can't be this mad at me. I can't take it." She dropped her head onto his chest and slid her arms under his shoulders, pulling him against her.

Matt's eyes stung as she hugged him tightly, and he lay unmoving while she clutched onto him. He should push her away, tell her again to go to hell, because keeping her at a distance might be the smart move. He didn't know anymore. Perhaps all of the choices he'd made since Finn's death had been the wrong ones. Matt didn't know who or what to trust, but he moved his hand to the back of her head and gently stroked her hair, trying to soothe her trembling.

"Shhh...." he said.

Matt was taken aback by how affected she was by what happened between them. Julie's pain was not just about Celeste. It was about him. "I'm the one who's sorry. I didn't mean any of the things I said to you. You didn't deserve that." It was true. She didn't deserve his hateful words when he was too cowardly to tell her the truth about anything. All she had been doing for months was to try to help.

She rested her cheek against his chest, still clinging to him, the warmth of her body against his bringing him relief and calm. Matt's hand traveled from her hair to the top of her tank, over the straps and just grazing her skin.

"I was awful," he continued. "Your relationship with your father is none of my business. Of course you love him, and you have every right to. What I said was unforgivable." Matt kept his hand on her, starting to touch her shoulders and her back. He hoped that she could feel his sincere remorse. "You're the best thing to happen to Celeste. She was lost before you got here. As if she didn't belong anywhere. You're saving her. I *never* should have said what I did."

"No, I pushed her too much," Julie said quietly. "And you. It won't happen again."

"You've been perfect. I wish I could tell you everything, but I can't. Not yet." It would happen. One day she would know everything, but not tonight. First they had to recover from this.

"I know. That's all right." Her hold on him stayed strong, but he could feel tension begin to ease from her body. Matt didn't take his hand away for a second.

After a few minutes, Julie shivered a bit.

"Cold?" he asked.

"Yeah. A little."

He slid his legs, and they moved together so that Julie was on her side, under the blanket with him, and resting her head in the crook of his hold. Matt stroked her arm, running his hand up and down, over and over. Her body pressed against his felt like the most natural thing in the world, and the way she fit against him as though they were made for this embrace was overwhelming. She took his hand in hers, intertwining their fingers, and squeezed.

He squeezed back.

"So we're still friends?" she asked.

Friends. The worst word. But he would take it, because it was the most important thing. "Yes," he said after a moment. "We're still friends."

Julie yawned. Their fight had drained both of them, and Matt wanted her to get some sleep. She had been through a lot tonight, too. And if she stayed awake any longer, she would come to her senses and leave. He slowed his touch over her arm and shoulder and listened to her breathing change as she drifted off in his arms.

If he fell asleep, he would miss this. So he stayed awake and spent the next two hours trying to memorize what her body felt like next to his. When the truth came out, when his many lies were exposed, she would hate him for what he had done to her. She was worth so much more than his cowardice.

If things were different, if he could go back and do this right.

If Finn hadn't died, if Celeste weren't so troubled, if his parents weren't withdrawn and stuck on compartmentalizing everything....

But Matt was the one to blame. He could have stopped this mess with Julie before it ever started. If he'd been strong enough.

Too many ifs.

"I'm so sorry," he whispered into the dark. Matt brought his lips to the top of her head and lightly kissed her.

Julie lifted her head slightly.

"God, I'm so sorry, Julie," he murmured.

"Me too," she said.

Julie raised her head more, bringing her mouth by his. He couldn't breathe. What was she doing? She couldn't be.... But she was, because she put her lips to his. They held still, delaying the moment that could change everything. They shouldn't do this. It would be a mistake.

Matt placed his hand firmly on her waist and pulled her up. And then he kissed her. Her lips were incredible, and their kiss gentle and unhurried. He moved his tongue against hers, and she pressed her mouth harder against his, her response heating up their connection. Then she slid her leg over his and pressed her waist against him, bringing them even closer together. Her body moved up, her chest now against him, and he put his hand to her lower back, raking his fingers against her skin. Julie slid a hand behind his head and pulled him in even more. The heat and the intensity between them grew. Too fast.

Matt didn't want to stop, and it was clear Julie didn't either. More than anything, he wanted to roll her onto her back, and to take this further. He would slowly ease off her clothes. He would hold his body over hers, kissing her for ages, only eventually pulling away from her lips to work his mouth down her neck, over her chest, her stomach. Lower. He wanted to make love to her, to show her how adored she really was.

Julie's breathing was picking up as he continued to kiss her, teasing her with his tongue, coaxing her into response. She wanted him, it was easy to tell. And he wanted her more than he ever could have imagined. This was not Julie with *Finn*. This was Julie with *Matt*.

He knew they could keep going. Given how she was moving against him, she wouldn't stop it.

So he had to. Because Julie with Matt was too complicated. She didn't know what she was doing. Her first time couldn't be like this. Matt would never do that to her. This was not about just sex, although she had to be aware of how turned on he was....

He squeezed her hand one more time and pulled from her kiss, resting his head back on the pillow. He looked at her as he tucked her hair behind her ear. It was good that he had just stopped things because he saw enough shock and confusion in Julie's eyes as it was.

She would probably come to her senses and leave now. Their fight, their horrible exchange of words out in the hall.... That was the reason for this late-night fooling around. It had to be. Feelings got mixed up in the aftermath of their fight. That was all. She loved the idea of Finn, not the idea of Matt.

But she didn't leave. She put her head back on his chest. Matt wrapped his arms around her. *Fall in love with me, Julie, as I fell in love with you*, he willed her. *Fall in love, fall in love, fall in love....*

Only for tonight, they belonged to each other, so he would stay awake.

Even if this closeness was just a result of mending what broke during their fight, he would take this excuse to stay next to Julie, the girl who had an irrevocable hold on his heart.

He would save her having to wake up with him. He wouldn't leave her until she started to stir. Then he would ease his body away, slip downstairs, and this would be over.

The Jump

Flat-Out Love, Chapter 32 retold

Matt Watkins Sometimes I feel depressed that I've wasted so much time, and I'm still no closer to discovering the resonant frequency of the human head.

Julie Seagle just "checked in" to your heart.

Years ago, Finn told Matt what he should do. *Let your world as you know it be blown to bits because you fall heart-crushingly head-over-heels for someone.* Matt had done that. And then he'd fought as hard as he could not to lose her that day last spring when Julie walked out of his life. He'd fought as *hard* as he could, and it didn't help. His conversation with Julie—when the truth came out and when he begged her to stay—played over and over in his head all summer. Her words kept him up at night.

This was never going to end well. You realize that, don't you?

And you're so broken.

And you hurt me.

We're not anything, Matt. Not after this.

You've broken my heart twice.

Nothing that happened has been true.

If you loved me, you couldn't have done this. You couldn't have been so careless with me. You know pain and loss and hurt better than anyone. And that's what you gave me. I know that it's not the same. I know yours is worse. I'm so sorry for you, Matt. For your whole family. You've all been through hell. And you've been braver than anyone could. But I hurt now too. And I can't love you.

Matt had kissed her, poured out his heart, pleaded with her to give them a chance. He threw everything he had on the table, and Julie left him anyway. Matt didn't blame her.

He wrote to her many times, hoping that communicating by e-mail would be easier and that he might be able to reach her. She was worth the pain it took to write her because he would never love anyone this deeply. The only response he got was one message asking him not to be the one to bring Celeste to any of the meet-ups with Julie. Eventually he stopped writing. He finally accepted that she would never love him.

So he let her go.

But then this morning, she came to Celeste's going-away party for Flat Finn. He knew she would be there, and he expected her to be tactful but cool. She wasn't a vicious person, but she clearly wasn't coming to the party for him. So he prepared himself to be as polite as she would surely be, and he also prepared to have his heart torn out again.

Instead she ran to him, right into his arms. Never had he been so shaken by love. And he heard words that changed everything.

I missed you.

It was always you. I thought it was somebody else, but it was you. You were the person I felt.

I love you.

I want to jump with you, Matt. For real this time.

The nightmare was over.

Right now, on what was turning out to be the most surprising and wonderful day of his life, Matt and Julie stood by the open door of the plane, the wind raging and the sky calling. She was strapped closely to him, her back pinned to his chest as they readied for their tandem jump. She looked adorable in her jumpsuit, helmet, and goggles, and her energy and excitement were palpable. He couldn't believe that she wanted to do this with him. And not just the skydive.

It was loud in the cabin, but he put his mouth to her ear. "Are you scared?"

"No!" she yelled above the noise.

He smiled. "Are you scared?"

"Yes! Yes, I'm scared!" Matt could feel her laughing against him.

"I'm here! I've got you!"

She nodded hard. She knew.

Matt looked to his left to one of the instructors he'd known back when he jumped with Finn. He got a smile and a thumbs-up, so Matt walked Julie to the edge. He had never been so happy. "Do you feel the rush? You feel it?"

It took her a minute, but she nodded. She had to feel it. The clear day gave them a spectacular and expansive view. There was no denying how high they were or what they were about to do.

The words he used as Finn came out. "You can do this. You're strong enough, and you're brave enough. You can do anything."

She nodded again.

Julie crossed her arms over her chest, just like she'd been taught in today's training.

Matt put his hand on her forehead and tucked her head back hard against his shoulder. "Here we go, tough girl." He grabbed the metal bar above and rocked them back and forth. One, two, three times.

And then they jumped.

The fall was smooth. It must be happening in slow motion, Matt thought. It was quiet, the ripping noise of the air nearly inaudible.

Matt could feel Finn so profoundly in this freefall. The grief was still sharp, yes, but he was equally affected by how much he just damn adored Finn and how unbelievably lucky he was to have had the brother he did. Not everyone gets that. Matt had Finn's love and playfulness and devotion when he was alive, and now, even after his brother's death, Matt still had those in his heart. That was something pretty damn beautiful.

With Flat Finn folded and secured in the pack on his back, Matt knew that this freefall was for Finn, for Julie, for Celeste, for his parents, and for himself. He floated with Julie, just the two of them in the infinite sky, as together they healed in the aftermath of devastation.

He didn't want it to end, but he was ready for the landing this time. "Hold on. I'm pulling the chute."

"Woo hoo!" Her thrill rang loud in his head and his soul. Julie loved this. And she loved him.

He yanked the cord, jettisoning them up briefly as the chute opened, then slowing their descent so that they drifted.

The view was gorgeous, and the landscape in Western Massachusetts came into focus as they floated over acres of green foliage and grassy fields. There was so much out there, and Matt had been lost in his cloistered life for far too long. No more. It was time to reconnect, to explore, and to dream again.

With Julie. Maybe they would travel this year? There were places to visit, new people to meet, experiences to savor. There was life to be lived.

"We're about to land, so get ready to run," Matt told her.

When the ground was just beneath them, they both started running in the air until their feet hit the grass. As they ran, the force of the landing threw Matt harder than he was expecting, and they fell forward. He caught himself on his arms just before his weight crushed Julie.

"You okay?" he asked.

"Hell, yes, I'm okay!" She was breathing hard, the exhilaration coursing through her system in the same way that it was for Matt.

He reached between them and undid the buckles that kept them together. He held himself above her, frozen, because this was the hard part. She wasn't strapped to him any longer. She could go.

Julie rolled onto her back under him and lifted off both of their helmets and goggles while she caught her breath.

"Matty." She smiled. "Hi."

"Hi."

"That was fun. Like, really, really fun."

"Good." Matt tried, but he wasn't able to smile with her.

She grew serious. "What is it?"

He couldn't answer.

She touched his cheek, studying him and reading him in the way that only Julie did. "Are you scared?"

"No."

She asked again. "Are you scared?"

"Yes."

"That I'll leave? That I'll get up and walk away?"
She was sending his own words back to him, bringing
their online life further into reality.

"Yes."

"I won't do that. I won't leave." Julie reached her
arms around his neck. "Close your eyes, Matthew,
and listen while I tell you how I feel about you."

He did what she asked.

"You are my everything," Julie said. "You are
challenging, and difficult, and guarded. I love those
things about you. You are fascinating, and complex,
and brilliant, and funny. I love those things about
you, too. I am in love with your selflessness and your
ability to sacrifice too much. I am in love with the
parts of you that fear and that hurt and that push
people away. I am love in with your vulnerability and
your strength. I am in love with your capacity to love
harder and with more loyalty than I ever imagined
anyone could. I am in love with the choices you've
made, even the mistakes, because they brought us to
where we are right now. More than those things, I am
very simply in love with you and everything that you
are. Your past, your present, and your future." She
touched her fingers to him, tracing his lips and then
moving across his jaw and over his cheek. "I think
about you all the time, and I can't get you out of my
head. I am listening to my heart, *finally*, without
doubting anything. And I will never stop." And then
she kissed him. Long and hard and endlessly, only
eventually slowing. "Now open your eyes and look at
me. I feel everything that you feel, Matt. I always
have, and I know that now. And it is time to stop
hurting."

Matt dropped his head and rested his cheek on hers, not caring that Julie felt the tears now pressed between them.

I did it, Finn. I did it. I was ready to jump, and now she's jumping with me.

Keep Going

Flat-Out Love, Bonus Chapter 33,
Julie's Point of View

Matt Watkins I will never compromise on my poorly-thought-out, internally-inconsistent, quasi-irrational principles. That's just how I roll.

Julie Seagle You are my favorite status reader in the whole wide world. Yes, you.

Celeste Watkins has no contractual obligation to use contractions. So maybe she will use them, and maybe she will not... So maybe she'll use them, and maybe she won't.

Julie leaned her head against the window and looked at Matt as he drove. He was clearly trying as hard as she was to keep from smiling. The effort was particularly adorable on his part, considering that he was not prone to walking around grinning at the slightest thing. It was wonderful to see him happy. Not that she didn't love his serious side. While Julie could be reduced to silliness at the mere mention of, for instance, any one of the Kardashians, Matt was more controlled. Controlled, disciplined, focused.

Not bad qualities for a number of things.

She shifted in her seat and drifted her hand over his thigh. Matt took a deep breath and gave her a quick glance before staring back at the highway in front of them. He tightened his hand over hers.

Aha! He was just as squirmy as she was.

"Why aren't you two saying anything? This is incomprehensible!" Celeste leaned forward from the back seat and popped her head between them. "There has been a major event, and it seems that it would be appropriate for both of you to be engaging in some sort of dialogue in which you detail the experience."

Julie couldn't stop watching Matt as she spoke. "I jumped out of an airplane," she said slowly.

"I know, Julie! You did, didn't you! It was an act of outstanding bravery, if you ask me."

"I jumped out of a goddamn airplane." She was aware that she was still reeling from the day. Still in shock. The last thing that she wanted right now was another rapid-fire conversation, but with Celeste around, avoiding that would be nearly impossible. Stringing coherent words together was simply not easy, though.

"Say more," Celeste demanded.

"I jumped out of a goddamn airplane with Matt." She paused. "Because of Matt. *For* Matt."

She heard him catch his breath. "Julie."

The sound in his voice now, the way he spoke her name....

There was a new tone there that she wanted more of. She could feel the ache between them now. The need. This morning she kissed Matt, threw her arms around him, and told him how totally wrong she'd been to walk away from him before. Then she felt that first surge of crazy heat that came after months of denying what they meant to each other. And now that they'd jumped from that plane together, Julie couldn't get over how deeply she trusted Matt.

Celeste sighed happily and sunk back into her seat. "I find that quite the romantic declaration. Yes, it's true that I may not be the utmost expert on romance, but I can say for sure that gestures like this must certainly be up there with Romeo and Juliet's. Although clearly those two died at the end of their story, and fortunately there was no glitch with your chute because here you are. Alive and well. Obviously."

Matt practically snorted. "Gee, thank you for that, Celeste. I bet Julie made cardboard cutouts of us, though. You know, just in case."

"Jesus, Matt," Julie muttered.

"Ha! I thought that was funny. Don't worry, Julie, I can appreciate some teasing regarding Flat Finn. Granted, that joke was still morbid and disturbing, but considering that has been my family's predominant theme for so long, I am quite comfortable with it."

Matt squeezed Julie's hand again. "You do know that we weren't going to die, right?"

"Yes, Matthew. Today was certainly not about creative suicide. At all. It was about us. Also," she said more softly, "I should point out that the day is not over."

The car picked up noticeable speed. "How many more exits until we're home?" he asked.

"Why are you in such a rush?" Celeste demanded. "It's only six o'clock."

"I just…. I just would like to get you back to the house."

"What about you? Won't you two be staying for dinner? I bet we could get Mom and Dad to watch a movie with us. Mom will probably try popping popcorn kernels herself in that idiotic oversized pot she likes so much, and we'll all be stuck eating charred nuggets, but it could be nice and representative of a highly functional family."

Matt cleared his throat. "I'm just going to drop you off, Celeste."

"Oh. Are you and Julie going somewhere? What will you be doing? There's a Greek festival in the South End this evening. That could be delightful, don't you think? Spanikopita, baklava, and lots of yogurt items, I imagine."

Julie grinned. "Is that what you were thinking, Matt? Are you in the mood for a little music and dancing? A tour of the Greek cathedral, perhaps?"

Matt raised an eyebrow. *"Tour the Greek cathedral,* huh? We can call it that, if you want. Sure."

Julie smacked his arm and then turned to Celeste. "We may get there. Matt is going to take me home so... that I can get cleaned up. I'm probably covered in dead bugs, so I need to decontaminate."

"Cleaned up? Decontaminate? Gee, you're full of euphemisms today, aren't you?"

"Matt, seriously," Julie said between clenched teeth and nodded toward the back seat.

"Don't worry," Celeste said with delight. "I'm following along just fine. I understand that neither of you will be attending the Greek Festival. And you two certainly have no business visiting any cathedrals."

****

Matt took the keys from Julie's hand, tossed them across the room, and shut her apartment door with his foot. He moved one hand behind her neck and pulled her mouth against his. She whimpered slightly, overwhelmed at how much she felt for him. The few kisses they'd shared before had been driven by emotion. This was different. This time it was about heat and longing. More specifically, how completely she wanted him out of his geeky *I'm Uncertain About Quantum Mechanics* T-shirt.

He pulled away for a moment. "Dana's not here, right?"

Julie shook her head. Dana was gone for the weekend, but she was having trouble finding the words to say so. To say anything.

She had just jumped out of an airplane.

And, as of a matter of a few hours ago, she and Matt were together. No more secrets between them, no confusion.

This day was a lot to take in. And she wanted more.

"Julie?" Matt asked.

Although she knew logically that her body was here in the apartment, part of her was still falling to earth, as if she were still in the jump. It had been just as Matt described it. A rush, a high, a drug. A degree of pounding terror, sure, but mostly a dreamlike, out-of-body, euphoric experience. One that she was still in. The straps holding them together for the tandem jump had been tighter than she had expected, but she'd liked that. Being so tied to Matt, becoming totally part of each other.

"Julie? You okay?" Matt tucked her hair behind her ears and looked at her with concern. She lifted her mouth to kiss him again, but he stopped her. "Are you... here?"

She put an arm around his waist and pulled him in. "I want to be with you," she whispered.

"I want to be with you, too. But you need to be grounded. You're still in the air, aren't you?"

"So what?" She smiled. "I like it up here. And I still know what I want."

"I need you to be here. With me."

She kissed him again, hard, and he responded with equal intensity, feeding her lightheaded state and letting her continue to drift in her soaring, dissociated world of rushing air and white noise. It was everything and nothing at the same time: feeling too much, too little, trying to separate this world from the adrenaline-based world. Eventually his kisses slowed, softened, and his firm hold on her waist eased a bit. Matt was bringing her back down to reality, gently and respectfully. And now that's where she wanted to be. She let clarity set back in.

Julie took her mouth from his as she wrapped her arms around his neck, hugging him tightly. "I'm here."

"In that case," Matt stepped back and began unzipping her sweatshirt, "you have on way too many clothes."

She put her hands over his. "Wait, I should go take a shower... first." She could smell the leftover stench of fear still on her skin from the skydive.

And maybe from what she knew she was about to do.

Matt smiled. "In that case, you still have on too many clothes. And I'm pretty sure you're going to need some help in that shower."

"Because I'm incompetent?" she teased.

"Of course not. But showering can be complicated." He dropped her sweatshirt to the floor.

"It's really not something you should try to take on alone after the day you've had."

Julie kicked off her shoes. "That's incredibly kind of you to offer your skilled help." She took his hand and led him down the hall to the bathroom.

Wait a minute. Oh God. What the hell was she thinking? The bathroom had bright lights. And a toilet. How sexy is a toilet? Not very. Unless you're into weird things. Which she wasn't. In fact, as a person who had never been entirely naked with another person, she didn't have the experience to be *into* anything. And what about the lights? Unless she's got some crazy supermodel body, no girl wants to be seen under a horribly unflattering glare. But now what was she supposed to do? Stop in her tracks, shove Matt back into the hall, and slam the bathroom door so that she could shower in privacy? That was stupid. Being naked was stupid. Sex was probably stupid.

But then they were there, about to be surrounded by tile and pornographic lighting. This was a terrible idea.

Matt hit the switch on the wall, and in what Julie was quite sure could only be a sign from the universe that Matt was the one—*her* one—the light bulb crackled and flashed before going out. She smiled. Now there was just early evening light filtering through the window.

It was time to stop thinking.

She turned on the hot water in the shower, and then Matt was behind her, pulling her against him. Ever so slowly, he undid the top of her jeans. She looked down, watching as he pushed them lower until they fell to the floor. His hands moved to the hem of her shirt, and she raised her arms as he pulled the fabric over her head. He pushed her hair aside and brushed his lips over her neck. The way he was moving his tongue over her skin made her knees weak, and she leaned her head back into him.

The sound of his voice in her ear made her shiver. "I have been thinking about this—about you—for months."

His hands moved to the curve of her waist, then up higher, gently over her breasts. For a moment, one hand slipped into her bra, tightening just enough so that she closed her eyes as a wave of anticipation took over. Steam from the running shower started to fill the room. Julie could feel her breathing pick up, her chest starting to pound under his hand. She nearly cried when he pulled away, but when that touch moved lower, down her stomach, the tips of his fingers sliding just under the top of her underwear... she didn't complain. As he traced the outline of the fabric so painfully, *painfully* slowly, Julie briefly wondered if anyone could literally go insane with lust. Not just because of what he was doing to her now, but because it made her wonder what he might do to her later. He was both careful and aggressive. He was in control. It was the same way that Matt managed so many parts of his life, with this same undeniable capability.

"You were scared earlier today. In the plane, before we jumped." He whispered in her ear and then kissed her shoulder. "What about right now?"

"Yes."

"Don't be." His hands slid over her waist, across her stomach, until she was fully embraced in his arms. He held her close. "We'll do what you want, when you want."

She turned around to face him.

How you find love means nothing. It's what you do with it when you see it that does. And when Julie looked at Matt, she unquestionably saw love. She would cart around hundreds of flat brothers and do the godforsaken Polar Plunge every year for the rest of her life if it meant that she would end up where she was right now.

"I want *you*, Matt. I want everything. You kept me safe today, you'll keep me safe now."

"Always. I promise, always."

Together, they eased off his shirt and pants. She took him by the hand as she stepped, still half-dressed, back into the shower, until she was leaning against the wall. Matt moved in front of her and pulled the shower curtain closed. She reached up for him, pulling him in to her, needing him to kiss her, to hold her. And he did just that. His kisses were so complete and passionate, so perfect, and she finally understood what it meant to drown oneself in another person.

She worried before about being self-conscious, about the lighting, about not looking like some airbrushed supermodel. That seemed a distant and ridiculous memory now because, considering how his hands were stroking her body, he made worrying about that impossible. And, she realized, he wasn't *that* kind of a guy. He didn't want or need her to be or look like anyone else. And she didn't need that from him. They were Matt and Julie, real people. That's why she could be so comfortable, so trusting, with him—he wanted her for who she was, as she was.

Soon his kisses traveled from her lips to her neck. Then to the top of her chest, getting harder, more urgent. Occasionally he'd pause in one spot, tasting her skin, savoring the connection between them. Julie reached behind her and undid her bra, now wet and clinging to her body. Before she could get her arms down, he had lowered the straps himself. She found her hands in his hair while his mouth moved over her breasts. Time started to get fuzzy. Then he was kissing her lips again as his fingers raked into her back, pulling her against his chest, driving her wild. Julie wrapped her arms around his neck, feeling as if she could never get him close enough. His skin was soft under the water... slick, enticing... and she started to let her hands roam. Soon her touch reached down to his waist and she pushed him away slightly so that she could finally get his underwear off.

He met her eyes as she fully undressed him, and that adorable, flirty glint of his filled his face. "Now there's just one more piece of clothing we have to get rid of."

He kissed his way down her breasts and stomach until he was kneeling in front of her. Julie wasn't sure how much longer she could stand up, and she couldn't help the noise that escaped her lips as he took his time getting off her underwear. How could anybody be so patient? Fortunately he was leading things here because she could have easily been convinced to skip all of these delightful steps and just... *Oh, God...* Matt stayed where he was, his hands caressing the backs of her legs as his lips kissed her thighs. Julie shut her eyes and ran her hands through her hair as he meticulously worked his way a bit higher. Then he stopped, staying where he was for an all-too-short few moments, before standing in front of her again.

"Matt...." she breathed.

While his tongue slipped inside her mouth again, he lifted her leg, resting her foot on the rim of the tub. Matt, Julie noticed, might be socially inept in a myriad of ways, but he was anything but inept now. Everything he did was effortless, smooth. His hand glided over her back, then down lower, pulling her against him for a minute, and then letting her fall away so he could continue gliding that hand to the top of her leg, to her inner thigh, between her legs....

Julie had to pull her mouth from his so that she could breathe. She dropped her head forward, resting against his chest as he worked his hand against her. Just as she was getting close to being as heated as she ever had with anyone, he stopped.

"No," she murmured, hearing the whimper in her tone. "Keep going."

He lifted her chin up, kissed her cheek, and put his mouth by her ear. "We're going to take our time."

She groaned, making him laugh. "But you said *what I want, when I want*. I want now."

He laughed again. "Trust me."

So, because she *did* trust him completely, she didn't protest as he washed her hair, soaped every part of her body, and teased her with lingering, unhurried touches. Besides, she knew that two could play at this game, so she returned the tease, taking the time to let herself get comfortable with him and with everywhere that her hands were starting to explore. It was impossible not to take a certain kind of satisfaction as Matt bit his lip when she let her hand graze between his legs.

She was surprised at how easy it was to be with anyone like this. She was... touching him. Quite intimately. Shouldn't she be more nervous? More self-conscious? But she wasn't. It didn't matter to her that she hadn't exactly been doing crunches and lunges all year in preparation for Matt seeing her naked because they were about more than that.

Later, in bed, Julie knew that no one had ever been so grateful to have the hot water run out. Not that she had anything to compare it to, but whatever Matt was doing with his tongue to her under the sheets right now was pretty unbelievable. Technically, what he was doing to her for the *second* time, but she wasn't about to bring numbers and math and geekiness into this. Although the thought occurred to her that, considering Matt took every conceivable thing to an outrageously academic level, there was an extremely good chance that he'd extensively researched female anatomy and become some sort of expert on the subject.

But since he was the first person to make her body tremble in a way that only she had made happen before.... Well, from now on, she would never complain when he got so engrossed in his laptop that he failed to hear anything that she was saying.

God, he was thorough and attentive in a way she couldn't have dreamed of. Julie moved her hand down, stroking his shoulder. She was nearly delirious.

But it wasn't just what he was doing to her physically that was making her so euphoric. It was him, being close with him. Trading touch, and sound, and taste with the person she cared so much for. How, even though she didn't know exactly what to do, Matt relaxed her, guided her, responded to her. Julie knew that for so much of their time together over this past year, she had been the one in control, steering him in different directions with Celeste, trying to bring him out of his own shell, and helping him find himself again in the craziness of his family. Now it was his turn to lead her, to be in charge, and she needed that from him. She liked that he was taking care of her. He would do what he was doing to her right now for the rest of the night if she let him.

And that one thought did interrupt her absolute bliss.

Julie reached her hand down and lured Matt up to her. She kissed him deeply, showing him how much she wanted him. "Matt?"

"Are you okay?" he asked.

"Matthew Watkins, are you stalling?"

"Am I what?"

"Are you stalling?"

"What...? Why are...? Do you want me to stop? Julie, we can stop anytime you want to. You know that, right?"

He sounded so cute and worried that it just confirmed her thought. "You *are* stalling."

Matt slid his arms underneath her shoulders and held her. He didn't say anything for a minute, but she had learned to wait him out. "Maybe a little," he whispered.

"Why?"

"Julie, until this morning, I thought that I'd lost you. That maybe I'd never even had you to lose at all. And now you're here, and...."

"Matt." Julie kissed him again, reassuring him.

He dropped his head, nuzzling into her neck. "I don't want to lose you. Not again."

"You won't."

"What if this changes things? What if we're moving too fast, and you flip out tomorrow, and that's the end? I don't want that to happen."

She lifted his face and made him look at her. The light from the hallway was enough that she could see how genuinely scared he was. Trusting—after being failed by so many, including her—must be incredibly hard for him. "This is not happening too fast. How could it be? We've been together in one way or another for a year now. I want this. I want you. I know without any doubt that I'm here right now for all the right reasons. And I know that you are, too."

"I love you, Julie."

"God, I love you, too. I do. I'm sorry about everything I said to you last spring. About *not* being able to love you. It took me a stupid amount of time to... to reconcile you and... Finn... as being all you."

"I know what a complete idiot I was."

"Stop. I'm not mad anymore in the least. I'm here now because I choose to be, not because I'm confused. I'm not going anywhere. Really. Tell me you believe me." He didn't say anything. "Matt, tell me that you believe me."

"I'm considering whether or not to believe you. I need to run an algorithm on this."

"That's not funny."

"You might be trying to trick me into sleeping with you."

"Is it working? Because I am *desperate* to sleep with you."

He was shaking. Not dramatically so, but enough. He was always so confident, preferring to change the subject than deal with what he didn't want to discuss, and it was so unlike Matt to ever be nervous. To react in a way that he couldn't control. She knew that he didn't like it, that it made him uncomfortable, and yet it was a side of him that she absolutely adored when he let her see it.

"Matt? Matty?" She curled her hips up into him. "I want to feel you."

He smiled now. "That's it. I don't care if you're tricking me or not, you just killed any willpower that I had left."

Julie sighed with relief. "Oh, thank God." She stretched out an arm and groped toward the floor by the bed. "There's a bag there. Can you get it?"

Matt propped himself up on one elbow and reached out, pulling a plastic bag onto the bed. He rustled with the plastic for a minute. "Look, Julie, I'm happy that you're an advocate for safe sex and all, but—"

"Oh, no. I didn't get the right ones?"

"Um, it's not that. You must have seventy? Eighty condoms here? I don't know what you've heard, but even the best of us have certain limitations."

"I know *that*. I just wasn't sure which kind you... liked. So I got an assortment."

Matt leaned in. He kissed her, then ran the tip of his tongue over her bottom lip. "Then I say we test out as many as we can." He pulled a box from the bag and lifted his body from hers.

Julie's hands were in her hair as she struggled to control herself while she waited out the excruciating seconds it took him. She couldn't stand having him away from her. There was nothing she wanted more than to be as close to him as possible, and these few moments were torturous. She could feel herself squirming on the bed, unable to control how nearly frantic she was for this. For him. Maybe she was supposed to be acting more... virginal... or something, but as she had said to Matt, they had already been having a relationship for many months. She was going to be as frantic as she wanted.

Then his body was above hers, his chest barely touching her as he held himself up on his elbows, keeping his full weight just off of her. Matt kissed her mouth, her cheek, her neck. "Thank you," he whispered.

"For what?"

"For letting me be your first."

"I wouldn't have it any other way."

He started to move inside her. Ever so slowly. Just a small movement at a time.

Julie arched her back and tightened her grip on his back. He stopped.

"Julie?" he asked softly.

"Yes. Don't stop. Please don't stop."

"I don't want to hurt you."

"You're not. Don't stop," she told him. She moved her hands to his lower back, pressing on him gently. She could feel her breathing pick up. It wasn't entirely true that it wasn't hurting her at all, but it didn't matter. He was perfect.

He eased further inside her and groaned, then pulled back a bit before sliding in even deeper.

She forced herself not to tense up, keeping her body relaxed so that she could take him in, because the small part of this that hurt was getting lost in everything that felt so right. She pressed her cheek against his. The touch she had on his back lightened, her hands starting to stray as she sought out more from him. He pulled out gently and started to find a rhythm, gliding in and out at just the pace she could take. Julie turned her head, slipping her tongue into his mouth. God, he was an amazing kisser. She flashed back to that night in his room, the first time that he ever held her in his arms and the first time that they had kissed. Both of them had had so many defenses up then, but it was hard to look back and not wonder how she could have let things between them stop that night. How had she not totally melted and made him continue to kiss her then? How had she not wrapped her body around his, taking everything that he could give?

Julie moved her hands between them, pushing against his chest. He straightened his arms, lifting up, continuing to rock his hips into her. She wanted to watch him now see how he looked as he made love to her. And it *was* love. She could see that in his eyes. Fine, there was lust there also, but it was the intoxicating combination of the two that was throwing her into sensory overload.

She looked down between them. He knew just how to handle her body, how to take care of her. She lifted into him, matching his rhythm. "God, Matt...."

He smiled softly at her.

"More," she told him, her voice barely audible. It was hard for her to talk now. "More."

Matt started to move faster, still steadily and evenly, but faster. She closed her eyes, letting herself drift into this. She ran her hands over his arms, his shoulders, his chest, starting to lose any bit of inhibition that was left. The only thing to do now was to let herself be pulled into this almost semi-conscious place, a place that held only the two of them and their craving, sensation, need. There was nothing else now.

They must have stopped the world. They just must have.

Julie listened to Matt. She could easily be overcome by his sounds. The small growl that escaped his lips as he started to grind harder into her. The change in his breathing that told her he was getting closer. The quiver in his voice as he said over and over that he loved her, that he wanted her completely, that she felt impossibly good. She wanted to stay like this forever. But with the way Matt was working his body against hers, she knew he was close. Julie wanted that so much for him. It didn't matter that it was beginning to sting and that maybe she was using her hands on his waist to pull him in more than she should. She wasn't going to slow down. After everything that he done to her and for her tonight, she wanted to give him as much pleasure as she could.

They were moving together now so smoothly. Julie wrapped her legs around his, and Matt groaned again, louder now. He slid one hand under her back, bringing them even closer together. "Matty," she whispered to him. Julie gasped as his whole body tightened. She listened to him, took in his sound and the way he moved against her as he started to shake. She knew she would never get enough of this.

Eventually, he slowed. The minute that he caught his breath, his mouth found hers again, and he kissed her while he recovered, staying inside her. Julie trailed her hands through his hair, cradling him, loving him.

Matt took his lips away and sweetly rubbed his nose against hers. "You're all right? I didn't... hurt you? I'm sorry if... God, you felt so... mind-blowing. Everything about you is totally amazing. I got a little lost there for a bit."

"I couldn't possibly feel better right now."

Still joined together, they stayed quiet, snuggling and drawing out the moments that came with the calm after the fervor. There would never be another moment just as significant and valued in the way this one was. They both knew that. They would find other moments—maybe even better ones—but none with the exact tone as this one.

Afterward, when it was time to leave that precious place, Julie glanced at the bag on the floor. "So, that's one down, seventy-nine to go?"

Matt laughed. "I might need a minute. I can't wait to go through your rather extensive collection, but I might need a minute." He stroked his lips across her collarbone. "But until then, I'm sure we could find something else to do. Besides, you might be sore?"

"A little," she admitted.

"Maybe I can help with that. For instance...." His mouth never left her skin as his lips trailed to her shoulder. She almost stopped him when he lifted his body so that he was no longer against her, but then those kisses found her breasts, later traveling down her stomach and not stopping until he was settled between her thighs. "If I were to do something very, very gently, perhaps I could distract you from any discomfort." Matt moved his hands underneath her, lifting her into him.

As much as Julie admired his outstanding genius when it came to everything math, computer, and physics-related, she was much preferring the divine application of his smarts when it came to other things.

"Yes. I... I think that might work."

And then they were both done talking.

About the Author

New York Times bestselling author Jessica Park mines the territory of love's growing pains with wit, sharp insights, and a discernible heat and heartbeat. Her previous novels include *Flat-Out Love* and *Relatively Famous*, and her NA book, *Left Drowning*, will be out July 16, 2013.

Please visit Jessica on her website, Twitter, and Facebook for the latest news and silliness.

Left Drowning, Coming July 16, 2013

Weighted down by the loss of her parents, Blythe McGuire struggles to keep her head above water as she trudges through her last year at Matthews College. Then a chance meeting sends Blythe crashing into something she doesn't expect—an undeniable attraction to a dark-haired senior named Chris Shepherd, whose past may be even more complicated than her own. As their relationship deepens, Chris pulls Blythe out of the stupor she's been in since the night a fire took half her family. She begins to heal, and even, haltingly, to love this guy who helps her find new paths to pleasure and self-discovery. But as Blythe moves into calmer waters, she realizes Chris is the one still strangled by his family's traumatic history. As dark currents threaten to pull him under, Blythe may be the only person who can keep him from drowning.

This book is intended for mature audiences due to strong language and sexual content.

Acknowledgments

Once again, Jim Thomsen provided lightning-speed editing and unfailing cheering throughout my writing career.

How Lori Gondelman catches the things she catches will always astound me, and I am in awe of her proofreading skills. Liis McKinstry and Maria Gowin also swooped in at the last minute to do final reads, and they are now stuck with me for life.

Without David Pacheco, my characters would be posting about weather and meals. So a big thank-you goes to Dave for writing all of the status updates for *Flat-Out Matt* and sharing a bit of his genius. Also for bailing me out and making me laugh. His ego will totally stay swollen for more than four hours now, but you should still follow him on Twitter @whatdoiknow.

Andrew Kaufman got me through tough writing days because he knows how to "listen to Jessica, damn it!" He also has quite the Celeste fixation, which both she and I enjoy to no end.

Tremendous, unrelenting love to In Like Lions for allowing me to use the lyrics to "Shallow Cars." James Bridges (guitarist and songwriter for ILL) wrote this gorgeous song, and I cannot recommend the band's music enough.

Massive gratitude to the entire team at Amazon Children's Publishing/Skyscape for the enthusiastic support they've given *Flat-Out Love*.

Most of all, thank you to my fans, whose Facebook and Twitter rallying for *Flat-Out Matt* absolutely stunned me. I could not have written this without you.